Ellie's Crows

Also by the author

Call Me Lydia
Maple Dale
Favored to Win
The Frog, the Wizard, and the Shrew
Maple Dale Revisited

Soon to be released

Hannah's Home

Ellie's Crows

MaryAnn Myers

Sunrise Horse Farm
11872 Chillicothe Road
Chesterland, Ohio 44026

First Edition
10 9 8 7 6 5 4 3 2

This is a work of fiction. Names, characters, places, and
incidents either are the products of the author's imagination
or are used fictitiously, and any resemblance to actual persons,
living or dead, events, or locales is entirely coincidental.

This book is printed on recycled stock & formatted to save paper.

Library of Congress Control Number: 2009900503
ISBN: 0-9668780-5-1

Sunrise Horse Farm is an organic, sustainable enterprise. It is an equine retirement sanctuary; it houses a bevy of dogs, and lives in harmony with the environment.

~ * ~

Permission to use an excerpt from "Becomings" written by Ellie King was granted by Moonwillow Press.

Thank you, Ellie!

*For asking her Grandpa Kramar which star is
ours, then a little girl and now a woman,
Ellie's Crows is dedicated to Jennifer Lynn.*

~ *Prologue* ~

The day Ellie was born; crows converged on the hospital and drove the pigeons away. The cooing outside turned into raucous cawing instantly. Ellie opened her eyes. There they were, all perched on the window ledge. The hospital was ancient. Ellie was ancient. She was an old soul, a friend, an enemy. "Taken before her time," they said.

She was back.

Ellie was different from the beginning. She knew early on life isn't always fair. "Crows can be violent sometimes, I hate to admit," she said, when she found blood on her hands one day. She was still a little girl, and had chased the crows away, but was too late. The sparrow lay dead. Ellie buried it near the oak tree next to the others, and went to school. Her teacher was a hawk. He smelled like dead leaves. No one knew this, saw this, and smelled this, but Ellie. She could see right through him. She made him nervous.

"Go wash your hands," he said.

Ellie refused. "The earth is my mother."

It was just this type of thing that made people talk.

"She's strange."

"She's weird."

When Ellie turned twenty, men appreciated her earthiness. She made them feel like wind. And fire. And water.

She made them want to live. She made them want to die.

She'd become a woman.

One doesn't become a woman overnight. Men might like to think that. But it isn't true. It comes day by day. It comes from standing in line. It comes from waiting on tables, from saying yes, from saying no, sometimes too much - sometimes not enough, and from burying the dead. When there are a lot of women in a room, it is crowded for more reasons than one. It is the past, and it is the future, and all the living in between.

Ellie was tired. She'd lived enough, and this time, wanted to get it right.

"Ellie?"

She turned and smiled.

"Can we go now?"

"Yes," she said. And the room was suddenly empty.

Ellie worked two jobs, lived okay, and was in love at age twenty-three. According to a lot of people, she was in love with the wrong man. From the time she could remember, she'd never been around a particularly bad horse. But men, that was a different thing.

She finished tacking Damian and led him into the arena. She had the place to herself, though she was never really alone. She glanced out the window. A flock of crows pecked their way about, all sleek and shiny black. Only one had its feathers ruffled at the moment. Probably Lolita, Ellie thought, her favorite of all the crows she'd ever known. She took a closer look. Yep, sure enough it was Lolita, named for the way every ounce of her....

"Ellie?"

She sighed, so much for solitude. There stood the farm owner's husband, Victor. "About your board."

"I'll have it tomorrow," Ellie said, and turned her back. She didn't like this man, didn't trust him. He reminded her of that teacher years ago. "Don't come near me," she willed in her mind. He stepped toward her.

"Can I give you a leg up?"

"No. No, thank you," Ellie said, as politely as she could. She mounted her horse and adjusted his girth. He had a habit of taking a deep breath and half holding it. She adjusted it another notch. Damian was a Thoroughbred Quarter Horse Cross; the best of two breeds. A registered Appendix Quarter Horse, he stood 16.2, all muscle and long legs, and was as black as Lolita. He was kind and gentle for the most part, but did have a streak in him that came out every now and then. Like the time he'd set out after that groundhog in the pasture. Ellie shuddered. He'd pawed at that crevice in the ground for the longest time.

"It's not that I'm worried," the man said, in that all too sleazy way of his.

Board was due the first of every month, and so was Ellie's rent. She always paid the rent first, and three or four days later, Damian's board. She was never any later than that.

"Maybe you and I can work something out."

Ellie ignored the suggestion. "I'll have it tomorrow." She'd been ignoring his suggestive comments for months now. His persistence was annoying. She had never ever encouraged this man. In fact, her behavior toward him was quite the opposite, and still, he would not leave her alone. Another boarder arrived just then, a friend of Ellie's. Thank heaven.

"If friends were money," Ellie's Grandma Betty would say, "you'd be rich." Grandma Betty was Ellie's best friend, and had been, ever since the day Ellie saw a robin land on her shoulder in the nursing home courtyard. Up until then, Ellie's visits had been obligatory. She'd never really known the old woman. Grandma Betty was her father's mother, the black sheep in the family, she'd been told. A hussy. A tramp and a thief.

Not so.

At least not to hear Grandma Betty tell it.

Ellie's friend Abby chased the man away with her mere presence. Several minutes later, she joined Ellie in the arena on her Hanoverian nicknamed Bubba for his size. The man sulked into the tack room and stood watching them through the crack in the door.

Abby was a novice, but what she lacked in experience, she made up for in zeal. "Oh look, there's Lolita," she said, bouncing happily against each of Bubba's commanding strides.

Ellie smiled. Lolita was bobbing her head up and down, as if posting to her own little trot of sorts. "Reverse," Ellie said, to see what Lolita would do. Sure enough, when Ellie and Abby turned, Lolita changed directions as well.

The man watched. When these two were riding out in the pasture once, a huge flock of crows followed them. Each time they stopped, the crows stopped, again and again, and would squawk and squawk as they landed all around. Usually something like that would spook the hell out of a horse, let alone a person. Yet neither seemed bothered in the least.

"Look at him," Abby whispered. "No, don't. Wait till I count three. One, two, three." They both turned their attention and for a second, a millisecond, the man was caught; his eyes beady like a hunter's at the end of a scope. As he walked away, red-faced, Lolita spread her wings in a magnificent display of black and purple.

* * *

Grandma Betty weighed eighty pounds and was literally starving herself to death. It was the only thing she had control over, she insisted. And she could swear like a sailor. "They're only trying to get you to eat," Ellie said, after she'd lit into one of the aides bearing a tray. "Here, drink your health shake."

Grandma Betty took a sip through a straw and handed the shake back. "There, I'll probably be around another whole day now."

Ellie smiled. "Make that two. Here."

Grandma Betty didn't fear death, nor did Ellie for that matter. They both knew they'd been on earth before, and at the rate they were going, since Grandma Betty had burned so many bridges behind her and Ellie had yet to cross the right one, chances are they'd probably both be back.

Grandma Betty slurped the rest of her health shake, and resigned herself to at least three, maybe even four more days now as a result. "I hope you're happy," she said to Ellie.

Ellie gave her a hug. "Did I tell you what the Dildo did?" 'Dildo' was Grandma Betty's nickname for Ellie's boyfriend Diablo, insisting that was probably all he was good for.

"No, what?"

"He bought a Harley."

"A Harley?" Grandma Betty made a face, her only acknowledgement to the news. "Check and see how many diapers I have."

Ellie got up and looked in the closet. She hated that term, diapers, and suggested in the beginning they call them something else. But Grandma Betty believed in calling a spade a spade. "Who would we be kidding anyway?"

Ellie counted. "One whole bag, and five, no, six in the other. Is that going to be enough?"

Grandma Betty sat thinking for a moment. "Should be. Do I still have powder? I think them girls take my powder."

"You have plenty." Ellie gathered up her grandmother's dirty clothes and put them in a bag. "Now remember I won't be here tomorrow. I have that dinner to go to."

Grandma Betty nodded. "It's about time the Dildo took you somewhere."

Ellie laughed and kissed her on the cheek. "I'll see you Sunday. Okay?"

"Okay."

Ellie looked back at her from the door, one last glance, always, ever since that time she feared she'd never see her again. "Fly, Grandma, if it be your will," she whispered. "If not, please eat."

"Bring me something," Grandma Betty said. "Something good."

Ellie promised she would, and stopped at the nurses' station on the way out. "Excuse me."

The floor nurse looked up.

"Someone's using my grandmother's powder again. It's almost gone, and I just bought it five days ago."

The nurse pursed her lips, started to say one thing and instead sighed. "I'll look into it."

"No," Ellie said. "Looking into it doesn't help. I want it stopped. That powder is hers."

"Fine. But are you sure she's not just dumping it out?"

"What?"

"Dumping it out? For attention. Sometimes for attention, old people will...."

Ellie glared down the corridor and raised her chin. "Don't make waves," she could hear her father say. "Your grandmother is on Medicaid. She's lucky they let her in there. You have no idea the strings I had to pull."

"Is there anything else?" the nurse asked.

"No," Ellie said, and turned on her heels.

*   *   *

Diablo asked Ellie to dance. The ceremony part of the evening had come to an end. All the awards had been handed out, the acceptance speeches made, all the "above and beyond the call of duties" accounted for. Now it was time to party.

Ellie looked stunning! Stunning being the word Diablo's Police Chief had used to describe her from across the room when earlier he and Diablo had met up at the bar. "Absolutely stunning! I wouldn't let her get away."

"She's not going anywhere," Diablo had said.

"Diablo...."

He held her in his arms. "Yes."

"There's something I have to tell you."

Diablo looked at her. "Good or bad?"

"Good," Ellie said. "Kinda sorta."

Diablo nodded. "Kinda sorta. I see."

Ellie smiled. He was doing his good cop, bad cop impression. He had the act down pat. He lived it: walked the walk, talked the talk. "It's about next weekend. There's this gathering out at Willenbrook."

"You mean the lesbian thing?"

Ellie chuckled. "They're not lesbians. Not all of them anyway. I'm going and I'm not a lesbian. Abby's going."

Diablo cocked an eyebrow. "Abby...? The Abby who looks-like-a-guy Abby?"

"She's married, Diablo. Married."

"Yeah, to Mister Twinkle Toes. I rest my case." He pulled her back into his arms, the music soft and romantic...his embrace, strong and intoxicating.

"I'm going, Diablo."

"Fine," he said, his mouth warm against her neck. "I'll see you there. Billings and I are assigned to the action."

5

"What?" She looked at him and saw he wasn't kidding.
"I'll be watching you," he said, along with a kiss.
Ellie just stared.

~ 2 ~

Abby was the one that always instigated their going to
retreats like this. "Something's missing in my life," she'd
said. "I don't know what, but I feel like that song. I just
know this can't be all there is." At least once, sometimes
twice a month, depending on the cost of admission and time
of day, out of curiosity, Ellie found herself being talked into
tagging along more and more. Willenbrook was their first
weekend overnighter.

"What on earth do they think we're going to need cops
for?"

"I don't know. I guess because of all the people planning
to attend."

Abby smiled. "Not people, women."

"What? You think women aren't capable of getting
rowdy?"

"Capable, yes. Probable, no."

The two hoisted their backpacks and sleeping bags and
took their place in line.

"I wonder what kind of food they'll have."

Ellie smiled. "Chocolate and cheesecake. What else?"

Those assembled ahead of them were rather quiet. "It's
almost an eerie kind of quiet," Abby suggested. "Feels
weird." It was dusk; the skies threatening rain, a stillness in
the air.

"Welcome, my sister," a woman standing at the
makeshift stockade fence entrance to the field said.
"Welcome." She took Abby's fifty dollars, stamped her
hand, and greeted Ellie. "Welcome, my sister. Welcome."

Ellie's hand-stamp smeared instantly with the first drop
of rain.

"Wonderful." Abby glanced at the sky and then surveyed
what used to be a field of maze "many moons ago"

accordingly and now nothing but a blanket of dandelions. "We should've brought an umbrella."

"Not allowed," someone behind them said very softly.

Abby headed straight for one of the Porta-Potties. "Oh look," she said, opening the door and pointing inside. "A candle. Cool!"

Ellie scanned the brochure for the umpteenth time since first laying her eyes on it months ago. No loudspeakers, no stage, no performances.

"This is just too cool," Abby said from behind the door. "Toilet tissue *and* Tucks!"

Ellie laughed quietly. There was even more of a hush in the air, and more rain, a steady drizzle. She scanned the horizon for a tree. None. Just acres and acres of dandelions, the blossoms all closing up for the evening.

Abby emerged, and they made their way to the already-forming circle of women. A classic flower child of a woman stood in its center, encouraging everyone to get comfortable. "Sit, please sit."

The ground was already rather wet.

"Sit...."

Ellie was the first to fold her legs and oblige. Abby second. The rest followed.

"Mother Nature is raining her glory upon us," the flower-child woman said, in the softest and most eloquent of voices. "Revel in her embrace." She raised her arms to the sky, swaying and encouraging all assembled to do the same, and smiled adoringly into the advent of night.

"If she starts singing Kumbaya, I'm gonna puke," Abby whispered.

Ellie glanced at her out of the corner of her eye, arms raised only slightly. Mother Nature was all around them, not just the sky. This was a mistake.

"There now," the center of their universe at the moment said. "Now that we have that silliness out of the way."

Everyone lowered their arms and broke into laughter. Even Ellie. Maybe this wasn't a mistake after all.

"Sit, sit. Come, come, all of you," the woman encouraged the latecomers. "Make room, make room. There is always room at Mother's table. Sit."

Ellie stared. Mother's table? Okay, so this was going to be a little corny after all.

"Now then." The woman wiped the rain from her eyes and steepled her hands. "First off, I'm going to ask you to turn to those next to you and bid them welcome."

"Welcome," Abby said, bowing from the waist in Ellie's direction, and then to the person on her right. "Welcome."

Ellie smiled. "Welcome to you, too."

"If you are comfortable, hug those around you."

Ellie and Abby chuckled and embraced. Abby was a hugger by nature. She hugged everyone within reach.

"If not, a handshake."

Ellie shook the woman's hand to her left.

"All of you are here for a reason," the woman said. "A purpose. Some of you may know that reason or purpose by the time you leave. Some of you may not. This could possibly be the beginning of your journey, or perhaps it is the end. Maybe it is just a stop along the way."

A clap of thunder roared in the distance.

"Some of you may rejoice."

Lightning flashed in the sky.

"Some of you may weep."

Thunder boomed louder.

"The only thing that is certain is that you will not leave this place alone. From this day forth, you will never be alone again."

Ellie bowed her head. Not in reverence, but in anguish, and sighed. "Bullshit."

"Bullshit?" she heard someone say. "Bullshit...?"

Ellie raised her eyes. All one hundred and three women in attendance, including the woman in the center and Abby at her side, were looking at her. And for once, Abby wasn't smirking or laughing.

"I'm sorry," Ellie said, the rain pelting her face. "It's just that there are times when I want to be alone. I don't think being alone is necessarily a bad thing."

The flower-child woman stepped closer. "But being alone *can* be a bad thing. It is in numbers that we survive. It is in numbers that we have a voice."

"Fine," Ellie said, embarrassed at being singled out. "We'll stick with the numbers."

"Come here," the woman said, extending her hand. "Come."

Ellie stood reluctantly.

"Come."

Ellie took the woman's hand. "Weep for those in pain," the woman chanted. "Weep for those in labor. Weep, weep, weep. Weep, sisters…weep."

Ellie started laughing. She couldn't help herself. When she looked at Abby, sitting there among all the supposed weepers, laughing as well, she laughed even harder. She laughed inside and out, the rain and the lightning and the thunder all around them. And finally, when she couldn't laugh anymore, she started crying. The woman released her to comfort and address each and every one. "Weep," she insisted. "Weep for one, weep for us all. Weep." The sky let loose with a torrent.

*   *   *

Diablo pulled the graveyard shift for this extra duty and arrived on the scene with his partner a little before eleven. "Well?"

The one cop being relieved shrugged. Nothing so far.

"What are they doing?"

"I don't know. It's dark back there. No lights."

"Is there shelter?"

"I don't know. Like I said, it's dark back there."

"Probably having an orgy," Diablo's partner said.

Diablo just looked at him.

"Probably naked women everywhere." He sniffed the damp air. "I can smell pussy a mile away."

Diablo took out his thermos. "That's because that's as close as you usually get."

The men all laughed, his partner included.

It was going to be a long boring shift, with none of the potential trouble materializing. No gate crashers, no protesters, molesters, no nothing. Just a beautiful clear sky with lots of stars now that the storm had passed. A peaceful night for them, and for the women.

Stripped down to her underwear, Ellie's waterproof sleeping bag was dry and cozy inside, the night air filled with warmth and promise. Tomorrow was going to be a better day. She heard a distant, contented, "Caw," and closed her eyes.

Someone tapped her on the shoulder. "Excuse me."

She turned.

"Do you have any dry cigarettes?" her intruder in the night asked. "I'm dying for a cigarette. Mine are all wet."

"No, sorry."

The woman moved on. "Excuse me," Ellie heard her whispering not fifteen feet away. "Would you happen to have any…?"

Ellie burrowed down and when she was comfortable again, dozed among the hum and buzz of hushed conversations everywhere. Abby woke at the crack of dawn and nudged her. "Rise and shine, Sister Bullshit. I smell bacon."

~ 3 ~

Halfway through the day, Ellie had doubts again. She'd never been raped, not even in a previous life that she could remember, was never abused that she could recall. She wasn't a cancer survivor. Her life wasn't a total shambles. She'd never been locked in a closet, or fed dog food; one shared story, was never harassed at work or shunned, lied to her whole life, or patronized. She'd never given birth. She was never abandoned, deserted for another man or woman, bore no physical scars. She wasn't even overweight. This was a waste of time. Hers and everyone else's around her, including Abby. Especially Abby, who sitting at her side, appeared to be having the time of her life.

"What? Tell me this isn't better than that guru guy when we all sat around with Paper Mache pyramids on our heads."

Ellie smiled. Abby had fun, no matter what.

"Besides, weren't those positively the best organically grown strawberries with farm-fresh whipped cream from 'penicillin and hormone-free' Jersey cows you've ever had in your life?"

Ellie laughed. "What now?"

Abby consulted the schedule leaflet. "Naptime." They made their way to their sleeping bags and got comfortable.

"Rest," the flower-child woman from yesterday said as she milled about. "Rest." She stopped and gazed down at Ellie.

Ellie shaded her eyes from the sun. "What?"

"I know you." The woman knelt down, touched Ellie on the forehead then her chin, and smiled. "I thought so," she said, before meandering on. "We've met before. And you were a non-believer then, too."

Ellie sighed.

First on the agenda after the nap, meditation. Ellie had just fallen asleep. "I'll do mine here," she told Abby. "You go on ahead."

Abby laughed. "No way, you're not leaving me alone. You see that lady over there."

Ellie turned.

"Well, she ain't no lady, if you know what I mean."

Ellie stared.

"I was behind her in line at the Porta-Pottie, and guess who left the seat up. It's a sure sign."

Ellie laughed. You could never tell if Abby was joking or not, aside from the time she fell off Bubba and right away said....

The meditation was guided imagery. "Breathe."

Ellie sighed. What was it with people, always wanting to tell you how to breathe?

"Breathe in through the nose and out through the nose. Visualize a golden yellow energy flowing through your being. Breathe...."

Ellie breathed, and heard a faint caw.

"Now close your eyes...."

Why, Ellie wondered? Why close your eyes? Why remove one's self from the physical world? She turned when she heard another caw, this one fainter than the first, different in tone, and gasped. "Oh my God. Lolita!" Her favorite crow was being swarmed by yellow jackets. Why on earth? Ellie jumped up, had to weave her way through the maze of women, and started running.

"Leave her alone! Leave her alone!" she screamed in her mind. "Leave her alone!"

The yellow jackets swirled and swirled, circling poor Lolita as she tried again and again to fly away, only to be attacked repeatedly - the buzz deafening as Ellie reached her. "Get! Get!" she shouted, batting at them with her hands. "Get!" She grabbed Lolita, her caw frantic and weakening, clutched her to her chest while swishing the yellow jackets, and remembered something long ago. "Get!" An attack, a former life, as a queen stood watching. The injustice. She hurried to the makeshift showers, gripped the handle, and with Lolita still clutched to her chest, turned the cold water on full blast. It drenched them both; Lolita's heart beat hard and fast inside her sleek shiny chest.

"There now," Ellie said. "You're okay. They're gone, you're okay. Be still. Be still...."

It was then Ellie noticed the crowd of women assembled all around her, watching, some with mouths agape, some with their hands clenched, in fear, in wonder, in pain, worry. And Abby, with tears in her eyes for Lolita.

The flower-child woman stepped forward, an expression of curiosity and anguish on her face. Ellie stared at her through the cascading water.

"I'm sorry," Ellie said, an apology for ruining the meditation, for their having to witness the violent display, disrupting everything, for signing up, for being there. "I'm different. I don't belong here. I'm not just a woman. I'm...."

"Alone," the woman said. "You are alone. You are alone because you choose to be. Where was her flock? Where is yours?"

Ellie swallowed hard and looked around. They were standing in front of her. The raped, the beaten, the mothers, the daughters…the dying, the surviving.

When the woman reached for Lolita, Ellie hesitated, and handed her over.

"Welcome home, our sister," the woman said, handing Lolita to Abby and embracing Ellie. "Welcome home."

* * *

Grandma Betty rang for the aide. It was a fifteen-minute wait, a rather quick response compared to usual. "A pain pill," Grandma Betty said. "I need a pain pill." A horrible searing pain was working its way up and down her arm.

"Which arm?"

"My right," Grandma Betty was careful to say. The last time she said the left, they carted her off to the hospital in an ambulance. "It's my right."

A half-hour later, the night nurse came in, took her pulse, then her blood pressure, 210 over 90, and said she'd be right back. Another trip to the emergency room. "For what?" Grandma Betty said. "I can die here just the same as there. A pain pill, please! My arm is killing me. No! No nitro, please! Please!" Grandma Betty spit the pill out.

The nurse returned with a nitroglycerine patch. "I'm sorry, Betty," she said, adhering it to her chest, the aide holding down both of Grandma Betty's hands.

"You're hurting me! You're hurting me! Let me go!"

"Relax, Betty. You'll be back before you know it."

"I don't want to go! I don't want to come back! Where's my granddaughter? Call my granddaughter! I insist you call my granddaughter! I have rights! You can't treat me like this! Nurse! Nurse!"

* * *

Lolita plucked a dandelion and flew away ceremoniously; a peace dove with an olive branch in her beak. Her flock could be heard cawing far in the distance, and then closer and closer in their approach, until they were all around them. The evening meal, the evening meditation was about to begin.

"Communion."

"Communion...?"

Ellie stared. She wasn't Catholic, Protestant either. Neither was Abby. She quickly scanned the brochure. Was this retreat church related? How'd she miss that?

It wasn't.

The communion was a form of intinction; a sacrament of bread dipped in wine. But not the body of Christ, his blood. This symbolic body, this blood, was womankind. "For sadly, my sisters, it is on this night, Saturday, that a travesty takes place. A mockery of the Sabbath. It is on this night most women are beaten and raped, murdered and maimed. It is on this night that their cries can be heard in the wind. It is on this night, for them, Mother Nature herself weeps. Let us join hands."

~ 4 ~

Ellie dreamt, or thought she'd dreamt, that in the middle of the night when all was still, she'd snuck out to the barricade, called Diablo's name, and melted into his arms. "What's going on, babe?" he'd said. "You wanting to feel like a woman?" She woke angry with herself, and angry with him.

But it was only a dream. It had to be. Diablo never called her "babe." Not only that, if it was actually real and not a dream - Abby would have yanked her right back at the start. Those were the rules; no bailing out at these retreats, no giving up, no giving in. "Walk this way.... Walk this way...." They were on a quest. It wasn't just the women on Oprah searching for their womanhood. There was a pilgrimage going on right here in the outskirts of little ole Sebago, population 52,000.

Ellie studied her right hand in the moonlight. She hadn't realized till hours after the attack, but she too had been stung, and numerous times. "Mud," one of the women had said. "You need mud."

"No, Aloe."

"Baking Soda."

"Calamine."

"Peppermint Oil."

Ellie used water. Cold water, and when it warmed from the fever of her flesh, more cold water. Until finally, the swelling subsided, along with the pain.

Grandma Betty called her name. "Ellie.... Ellie...."

Ellie stared into the wind. "Abby. Abby, listen. Do you hear that?"

"What?"

"Listen."

"Ellie." She heard Grandma Betty call her name again. "Don't come see me. I'm gone."

"Gone?" Ellie sat up in her sleeping bag.

Abby looked at her. "Who's gone?"

"Grandma Betty. She says she's gone."

Abby frowned. "Gone where?"

"I don't know. Gone, gone. Where else?"

Abby yawned. "You're dreaming. Go back to sleep."

Ellie looked at her. Another dream? Of course. Why else would she think she could hear Grandma Betty so far away? Or that Abby would either for that matter. Ellie herself had never heard voices before, let alone Abby. It was only yesterday that Abby rolled her eyes in utter disbelief when some woman started talking about "corresponding" with her dead husband.

"Go to sleep."

Hours later, when Willenbrook officially ended, with all the women hugging, exchanging addresses and phone numbers and bidding one another good-bye, some farewell, Abby headed for the barn, and Ellie the nursing home.

Grandma Betty was indeed gone.

"They took her to the hospital," one of the aides said, walking into the room and finding Ellie sitting there, obviously in some kind of shock, what with the way she just kept looking around the ceiling.

"The hospital? Why?"

"Her heart. She's fine though. They say she's coming back tomorrow."

Ellie sighed. Grandma Betty hated the hospital even worse than the nursing home. She could only imagine the mood she was in, the fit she threw. Ellie gathered a few of her grandmother's things, things she knew she'd want, and drove to the hospital. She'd promised Diablo she'd come straight to his apartment from the nursing home, but that would have to wait. She didn't want her grandmother any more upset than she probably was already.

Ellie entered the hospital room smiling, best foot forward, and stopped cold. Grandma Betty was strapped to her bed, restraining gauze everywhere. Oh God, Ellie thought as she stepped closer, tell me they didn't drug her.

Sure enough.

"Kemoran."

"Kemoran…? But she's allergic to Kemoran."

"Not according to her chart. Why, what happens to her?"

"It knocks her out. That and when it wears off, she becomes disoriented."

The nurse concurred, hence, why they'd had to restrain her. An orderly had caught her trying to climb out of bed, asked where she was going, and she said she'd just phoned for a taxi and was headed for the American Legion Hall. That there was a big dance there tonight, and….

Ellie smiled. That was Grandma Betty all right. Rumor had it she could party for days on end. "Would you please call her doctor and get him to remove the Kemoran. She'll ask for it again, and when she's had enough in her…."

The nurse made a notation on her clipboard. "I'll phone him shortly."

Ellie looked at her. "When is the next dosage due?"

"Well." The nurse scanned the chart. "She just had her third shot about an hour ago."

Ellie stared. Three? "Could you phone the doctor now please, before…?"

The woman heaved a sigh. "Sure."

Ellie thanked her and walked back into the room. Grandma Betty never even stirred. "Grandma." Ellie leaned close. "I'm going to go home for a while, but I'll be back. I brought your tissue." Her grandmother hated hospital tissue.

"I brought your comb and your powder and your lipstick. And I brought your housecoat and slippers, too. Okay?" She studied her grandmother's face, searched her closed eyes, her hands, anything for a sign that she'd heard, understood. Nothing. "I'll see you later, Okay?" She kissed her on the cheek and felt her grandmother twitch, hesitated, and then walked out. She needn't look back from the door for fear she'd never see her again. There was no way Grandma Betty would die in a hospital. It wasn't in the cards.

"Ellie."

Ellie turned, somewhat startled.

Her grandmother lay still.

"You're a good granddaughter."

Ellie stared, knew she'd heard what she heard, would have sworn she heard what she heard. But how? Her grandmother just lay there.

"Ellie."

Ellie glanced past Grandma Betty and almost fainted with relief. It was the woman in the next bed talking. A woman she'd never met, and yet…. "Your grandmother told me all about you yesterday. She said you were going to come and straighten everyone out here and get them to send her home."

Ellie smiled, but in the midst of that smile, she gazed at her grandmother lying there, helpless and waiting, depending on her, and here came the tears. "I'll be back," she said.

The woman nodded. "I know. Your Grandma knows, too."

Ellie waved, too choked up to speak, and out in the car, broke down completely.

*   *   *

Diablo opened the door and just stood there. He loved Ellie. There was no denying that. But at the same time…. "Well, you're only three hours late," he said, stepping back for her to enter and following her with his eyes. "What's your excuse this time?"

"None," Ellie said, plopping herself down on his couch. "None. I went to the nursing home, then the hospital, then the barn."

"I see," Diablo said.

"Damian has a puncture wound, three of them in fact."

Diablo closed the door and gave her that aggravated look he had down pat.

"Diablo, don't," she said. "All right?"

He held his hands out, implying he wasn't doing a thing. "I'm sorry. Okay?"

Diablo walked past her into the kitchen, grabbed a beer out of the fridge and with an angry twist, popped the lid and threw it into the garbage can.

"Fine," Ellie said. When he got into one of these moods, there was no talking to him. "I'll see you later."

Diablo hailed his beer, a sarcastic good-bye of sorts, and Ellie walked out.

She'd had every intention of going straight to Diablo's from the hospital, which would have put her there a little earlier. But when she'd had to drive right past the barn and Abby's car was still there, which didn't make any sense, since she said she was only stopping for a minute on the way home....

By evening, Grandma Betty showed signs of withdrawal and was somewhere in between the confused, frightened, and borderline paranoia stage. "These people are mean here, Ellie. Don't let them treat me this way. They want to put a tube in me. You'd better go talk to them."

"I will, Grandma," Ellie said. "I will."

"They want to send me to the hospital. I told them I'm not going."

Ellie nodded. She obviously thought she was back at the nursing home.

"Don't let them send me there, okay? Promise me you won't let them send me there."

"I promise," Ellie said.

Grandma Betty pulled hard against the restraints on her wrists. "I don't know what's happening, Ellie. Do you know what's happening?"

Ellie hesitated. "About what, Grandma?"

"This house. The way it is." Grandma Betty looked around the room. "Did you ever see such a mess? How'd it get this way?"

"I don't know, Grandma," Ellie said.

"Me neither." Grandma Betty leaned her head back. "But I'll tell you what, Ellie. I'm too old, and too tired to clean it anymore."

"Me, too," Ellie said, agreeing with her, which was always a good thing to do when she got like this. "Me, too."

~ 5 ~

Later in the day, Ellie went over Damian's stall from top to bottom. There were no nails sticking out, no splinters, nothing hidden in the sawdust. Nothing anywhere. So how did he get the puncture wounds? And three at that?

Abby held onto his halter while Ellie dabbed ointment on the affected areas. "Do you think you should call Dr. Oakley?"

Ellie shook her head at first, then shrugged and sighed. If she waited for him to just show up, which he did sometimes, depending on what was going on in the barn, she wouldn't have to pay for the farm call. And with money so tight.... "I think I'll just hang around for awhile."

"You sure? Do you want me to stay?"

"No. Thanks." They weren't alone. There was a lesson in progress, some people just finishing up, some regulars due to come, and no real reason for Abby to stay. "You go on." Abby and her husband were having company for dinner, and she had yet to decide the main course.

"That's the beauty of being a vegetarian," she'd said earlier, day two of her being a vegetarian third time around. "The entrée could be the peas, and who'd know otherwise?"

Ellie smiled. "Don't forget to save me some of the Tiramisu."

Abby nodded, and took a closer look at the one puncture wound lowest on Damian's hip. "Do you think he'll get proud flesh?"

"Go," Ellie said. "Just go, okay. Doomsayer."

Abby smiled, stopped to chuck Bubba on the nose when passing his stall, and was gone.

Ellie stared at Damian, wondering if maybe she should take him for a walk. He wasn't stocking-up; a condition where the legs swell, but could very well start. She hooked the lead shank onto his halter and led him outside. It was dusk. No sign of the crows.

Damian pushed up against her, rooting for a carrot. She didn't have any. "Tomorrow. I'll bring you some tomorrow." She led him down the path and over to the south-side paddocks. She stopped to let him graze a little, then walked him up and around the foaling barn and then down behind the utility shed, and was just starting back up toward the main barn, when she saw Victor, the owner's infamous husband.

He stopped what he was doing and just looked at her, watched her, watched her every move. She had nothing to say to him. She'd already questioned him about Damian's injury; had he seen or heard anything, was Damian cast, what? She walked on. By the time she put Damian back into his stall, the lesson was over, and the place was thinning out. No vet. She had another hour or so before she had to be at the laundromat where she worked part-time, had already been to the nursing home to visit Grandma Betty, who was transferred back today and still suffering the effects of the Kemoran. She had the time to wait longer, but.... She thought of Diablo, still angry with her no doubt, thought of that brooding way of his; that look. And the way, when all was well between them, how that brooding look in his eyes would change, and she'd want to be devoured by them, by him.

"Hi, Ellie!"

Ellie turned and smiled, recognizing the little voice. It was one of the twin girls who owned the pony stabled the other side of Bubba. "How are you doing?"

"Okay. You gonna ride?"

"No, not today. You?"

The little girl nodded. "As soon as the vet gets here.
Mom!" she called. "Mom!" And off she went to look for
her. Ellie decided to wait it out and when the vet arrived and
had treated the pony, walked down and asked him if he
wouldn't mind taking a look at Damian.

"No problem," he said, and followed her. Damian
pricked his ears. Still hoping for a carrot, Ellie figured.
When he backed up uncharacteristically as they entered the
stall, she chalked it up to his disappointment and pouting.

Only one of the puncture wounds concerned the vet. It
was pretty deep, he said, and already showing the beginning
signs of infection. He flushed it out, gave Damian a Tetanus
booster and a shot of antibiotics, and left a different type of
ointment to be applied twice a day.

"Is it all right to ride him?"

"Oh, sure, exercise'll do it good," Dr. Oakley said. "Just
don't get him hot. Take it easy for a few days. I'll check on
him Friday."

Ellie thanked him, put the salve in her tack trunk, and
walked as far as his truck with him, then on to her car. With
a little luck, she'd be right on time for work. As it was, she
was two minutes late, but two minutes was close enough.
The laundromat was packed with the night crowd, mostly
college students, a few couples with babies, an elderly man
who lived upstairs and washed a load a day, mixing whites
with colors. It was her job to make change and keep the
peace. Keep the peace? The worst that had ever happened: a
food fight between two slightly intoxicated freshmen, and
Ketchup everywhere!

It was customary for Ellie to close the laundromat
around ten. She never felt threatened or frightened. It was a
nice neighborhood, nice people, well lit. She glanced up
from helping Mr. Franklin fold his sheets when a hush of
sorts fell over the room, a silence amidst the swish of the
washers and tumble of the dryers.

There stood Diablo, his cop car parked right outside.

"Can I talk to you a minute?" he said.

Ellie swallowed, took him in at a glance, and nodded. "All right." She motioned to the back.

"What's the problem, officer?" Mr. Franklin asked.

"No problem, sir."

"It's okay," Ellie said. "I know him," she added. "He's uh…he used to be my boyfriend. I'll only be a minute."

Diablo followed her into the back room and when she turned to face him, again Ellie took him in entirely with a glance, gun on his hip, smoldering look in his eyes. For a moment he just looked at her. "Used to be?" he said.

Ellie wet her lips with the tip of her tongue and shrugged. "How many times can you get mad at me, Diablo? How many times before…?"

"As many as it takes," he said, stepping toward her. "As many as it takes." He touched the side of her face with the back of his hand and leaned down and kissed her, gently at first, then more urgently. "I want you," he said. "I want you now. I want you tonight. And if you don't make it to my place, I swear I'll come looking for you."

"Then what?" Ellie said, her mouth against his. "Then what, Diablo?"

Diablo kissed her again and looked into her eyes. "I'll show you, Ellie," he said, spreading her hand and running it down the front of his pants. "I'll show you. How about you just be there, all right?"

"Ellie?" Mr. Franklin called. "Ellie, is everything okay?"

"Yes, thanks. The officer's leaving."

Diablo walked out first, holding Ellie's hand behind his back. When he let go, he pointed at two teens sitting on the folding-table, who jumped off instantly. Ellie watched Diablo get into the cruiser, watched as he reached for the scanner, and looked at her watch. One more hour.

~ 6 ~

Grandma Betty dreamt she drowned, not once, but three times during the night. First in a river, then a clear warm pool the size of a small lake, and then a tub. She woke with a rattle in her chest and later that day was diagnosed with pneumonia.

"No more swimming," she told Ellie. "It just ain't worth it anymore."

Ellie smiled, held her hand, and turned to the nurse. "Will she have to go to the hospital again?"

"I'm afraid so."

Grandma Betty shook her head vehemently. "No. Ellie, go find me a chain. I'm gonna chain myself to the bed. I swear I will."

Lolita squawked outside the window.

Ellie ignored her.

"I probably got the damned pneumonia in the hospital, and now you want to send me back."

"You'll need to be put on antibiotics."

"So. What's wrong with giving them to me here?"

Ellie turned to the nurse.

The woman shook her head. "She'll need an IV, and in order for it to be covered...."

Ellie nodded, understanding; the Medicare-Medicaid thing. She sighed, and edged closer to Grandma Betty's bed. "It's all right. It'll only be for a few days." Three to be exact. It was always three, the customary three, the required three.

"Easy for you to say," Grandma Betty said. "You have your whole life ahead of you."

Ellie chuckled and gave her a hug, then sobered. Grandma Betty's skin was on fire.

Diablo wasn't happy when Ellie phoned with the news she'd be late.

"Is it too much to ask to be first on your list, just once?" he asked.

"Yes. It is. Until Grandma Betty dies...."

"That's sick. You should hear yourself."

Ellie smiled. "I do hear myself. I'll call you later. I gotta go, the paramedics are here."

"Are they cute, Ellie?" Grandma Betty wanted to know.

Ellie glanced down the hall. "Yes, very. Now what do you want packed?"

"Everything. I'm never coming back. I'm going to give up and die in the hospital. I'll show 'em."

"Who?"

"The nurses. The aides. The goddamned cooks. All the sons o' bitches! All of them!"

Ellie chuckled again, and would have laughed had Grandma Betty not been so pale and flushed, and started putting things in her three-day bag. Slippers, diapers, always her own, (she hated the ones at the hospital, said they itched like the dickens and made her squirm in bed) and floss, Grandma Betty still had all her own teeth, and....

"Ellie?"

"Yes, Grandma." Ellie turned.

A stillness settled around them. "It won't be long now, you know."

Ellie stared.

"I'm sorry. But it won't. Okay?"

Ellie steeled her jaw and nodded. "You did say it was all right for me to mourn though, right.... Remember?"

"I remember." Grandma Betty reached for Ellie's hand. "I remember. Just don't mourn too much. It'll mean regrets. And you and I, we have none between us. I wouldn't change a thing."

Ellie wrapped her arms around Grandma Betty and, hugging the frail little woman, fought back tears. "I'm sorry. I won't make you eat anymore. I promise."

"And the tubes?"

"No tubes."

Grandma Betty nodded gratefully and held her tight. "I love you, dear. I love you more than life itself," she said, and for a moment, a brief moment, she allowed her granddaughter to cry. And to cry herself.

*   *   *

As a rule, Ellie would never think of going to the barn late at night, not this barn, let alone by herself. But Damian needed to be treated. She parked her car out front instead of at the side as usual, visible from the road, and opened the large arena door. With the full moon at her back, showing the way, she quickly covered the distance to the stall area.

"Well, look who's here," she heard an inebriated male voice say. "What do you think you're doing?"

Ellie fixed her eyes on the couch outside the tack room, the owner's husband coming into focus little by little. Boots, then his jeans, open shirt. "I'm here to check on Damian," she said. Groping for the switch, she turned on the lights.

The man shaded his eyes and sat up, watched as she passed, and reached into his pocket for a cigarette. "You need help?"

"No," Ellie said, and kept walking. Damian was lying down and had to first be coaxed to his feet. She spread ointment on the puncture wounds, probably should have washed them first, probably should have taken him out for a walk as well, but not with Victor there, and this late at night. She reached into the bottom of her tack trunk for a bag of carrots, broke one in half, put it in Damian's feed tub, and turned, startled to find the man staggering there at arm's length.

"Go away," she said.

"What?" He laughed.

"I said, go away."

The man drew hard on his cigarette. "I was just coming to help."

"I don't need any help," Ellie said, adding, so as not to provoke him. "Thanks anyway." She started past him, and swung around when he brushed her arm.

"Whoa! Well, lookit here!" He stumbled back a step, amused at her reaction.

"Don't touch me," Ellie said. "Don't *ever* touch me."

"Right." He laughed as if she were kidding, moved toward her, and it was then that Ellie turned and summoned into the night for help.

"Come! Come now!" she cried.

The man looked at her. She was standing with her arms raised, eyes wild....

"Come now!"

Victor let out another laugh, a laugh that in the next instant turned mute with a face of its own as a flock of crows swooped down on the arena. They entered in droves...circling and circling and cawing and squawking.

"You're a fucking freak, you know that," the man said, backing up amidst the flutter of wings and stirring in the stalls. "A fucking freak!"

"What the...?"

Ellie turned to find Sheila, the farm owner, standing in the arena doorway, pajama-clad, and ducking and swatting at the birds with a gun in her hand.

"What's going on?" she yelled.

"Nothing," Ellie said, walking toward her and talking fast. "I had to put my grandmother in the hospital again, and couldn't get here sooner to treat Damian. I'm sorry, I didn't know Victor was here or I wouldn't have used the arena." Ellie waved her arms, shooing the crows, and one by one, they flew back out, cawing and cawing. "There's a storm coming, that's all. They were just drawn to the lights. Right, Victor?"

When she looked at the man he nodded. "Right."

Sheila lowered her gun as the last crow, Lolita, descended, and turned her attention to her husband, a man fifteen years her junior. "What the hell are you doing down here? I thought you were in bed."

"I was checking on that Dun mare. She looked colicky earlier."

The woman stared a moment and then smiled, a smile that to Ellie said he could do no wrong in her eyes. "Well, if she's all right, then come on. You must be tired. Let's go back to bed."

Victor nodded and walked past Ellie by way of a huge circle.

"Is it all right if I exercise Damian a bit?" Ellie asked.

"Sure, go ahead," Sheila said. "Just don't forget to turn out the lights."

"I won't. Thank you," Ellie replied. At the door Victor glared at her. This was not over between them. It couldn't have been clearer had he said it. It was in his eyes, in his posture, in his being, and apparently, though looking straight ahead, Sheila noticed it, too. She raised her gun and fired into the night. A warning shot!

~ 7 ~

Grandma Betty hummed in her sleep; a habit that drove all three of her husbands crazy. Ellie found it endearing. "Grandma."

"Yes."

"You were saying...?"

Grandma Betty opened her eyes, joined the living again. "That's right. Let me see, where was I?"

Ellie consulted her note pad. "Your ruby broach."

"Oh yes. I want that to go to Eloise."

"Eloise? I thought you didn't like Eloise."

"I don't," she said, and smiled. "But it ain't *really* a ruby, so...."

Ellie laughed. "Okay, that just leaves your pearls."

Grandma Betty nodded. "Now those are real." She paused and drew a short breath. "Give those to your mother."

"Okay." Ellie wrote her mother's name "Jewel" next to the pearls and turned the page. Going over the funeral arrangements was next.

"Cremated."

"Check."

"Ashes scattered."

"Check."

"As far as you can go in a day."

"Check."

"And no speeches."

"Got it."

"I mean that," Grandma Betty said. "Promise me."

Ellie nodded. "I promise." Done.

Diablo was in a good mood when he picked up Ellie on his brand new Harley. It would be just him and her and the open road.

"Can we stop at the barn first?"

"Why?"

"I have to check on Damian."

Diablo had been to the barn only one other time, and had taken an instant dislike to the horse. The damned thing had charged at him and no matter what Ellie tried to say afterwards, he insisted the horse had it in for him.

"Here, he's sorry, see...." She tried to get Diablo to give him a carrot.

"No thanks," he said. And that was that.

The barn and arena were all lit up as Diablo downshifted and turned onto the drive from the highway, the night air warm. "I love you," she whispered in his ear, thanking him.

"Five minutes," he said, turning off the motorcycle and leaning forward slightly so she could climb off.

"Aren't you coming in?"

"No."

Ellie laughed. "All right, I'll be right back."

Damian was happy to see her, as always, and nickered at the sound of her voice. She went into the stall to check his wounds, which appeared to be healing nicely, fussed over him and hugged and kissed him, and when patting him on the neck as she turned to leave, noticed something in the corner. Manure had been piled under his feed tub. She glanced at the back corners. It was piled there, too.

Victor.

It had to be.

When she finally returned, Diablo asked what took her so long.

"Nothing," she said, and climbed onto the motorcycle behind him. "Let's go."

* * *

Grandma Betty rang for the nurse; not her favorite, but one she liked okay and who would maybe take the time to talk, if need be. "I'm feeling rather strange," she said to the woman.

"Strange? How?" the nurse asked, checking her pulse.

"I don't know. It's hard to explain. Never mind." She pulled her arm away.

"Are you sure?"

"Yes." Grandma Betty raised a trembling hand to her forehead. "Never mind."

It was after midnight. The nurse turned to leave.

"Wait! Can I ask you something?"

The nurse nodded and pulled up a chair.

"It's about Mr. Porter. I hear he died. It that true?"

"Yes. This morning at o-six hundred."

"O-six hundred." Grandma Betty laughed, something about that striking her as funny. She'd forgotten that this particular nurse used to be a WAC, a former sergeant. "Well, the thing I wanted to know was, was he alone when it happened?"

"Alone. No. Mr. O'Brien was in the room at the time, and...."

"No, that's not what I mean. That old coot isn't company to anyone. He don't know up from down."

The nurse smiled, agreeing. "I think I know what you're asking Betty. You mean, was there someone sitting with him? A family member maybe."

Grandma Betty nodded.

"No. No one."

"Not even a nurse?"

"No, you have to understand, that's a pretty busy time for us nurses. It's just before the shift change and we joke about patients dying most often right about then, just to muddy our day, and...." She paused. "I'm sorry. Why did you ask?"

"Just wondering. Thank you."

The woman nodded and stood to leave. "Anything else? Can I get you anything?"

Grandma Betty shook her head. "No. But tell me, you say most people die in the morning?"

"Yes. And if it'll make you feel better, we do try to be with a resident when their time is near. It just doesn't always work out that way. Are you afraid you'll be alone? Is that why you're not sleeping?"

"No. My granddaughter will be with me when I die. I just wanted to give her an idea what time."

The nurse looked at Grandma Betty and smiled. She felt a little sorry for this granddaughter. Betty was too demanding of the girl in her opinion, had her jumping through hoops half the time.

"Are you frightened, Betty? Is that what this is about?"

"No, not at all. I just want to make sure I do it right."

*   *   *

Diablo came around from in front of the ice cream stand with two double-dipped chocolate cones and handed Ellie hers. "Taste," he said, and waited, watching. "Well, what do you think?"

Ellie let the chocolate melt in her mouth. "How do you find these places?"

"Slow nights," Diablo said, and Ellie laughed. That was his answer for just about everything. They'd had such a nice ride. It was a little after midnight. They'd be heading home now; his place probably, and hadn't had one fight or even a glimmer of an argument. Ellie was liking this Harley more and more. It was almost impossible to argue on a motorcycle.

"Diablo, why do you think we fight anyway?" she would like to ask, just once when he was in a good mood. But then that would almost certainly put him in a bad mood. She could see him throwing his cone in the trash, see him starting the motorcycle with sparks flying out of his feet, see him....

"You're melting," he said, and nudged her hand closer to her mouth.

Ellie licked around the sides and top and reached for one of the napkins tucked in his shirt pocket.

"You know why I love you, Diablo?"

30

"No, why?"

Ellie hesitated. A split-second ago, she knew. Now she had no idea, aside from the fact that everyone told her she shouldn't, that he was bad news and that she should steer clear of him. Don't give him the time of day. He's trouble. "Lots of reasons."

"Name one," Diablo said. "And don't say it's because I'm a good lover, because that I already know."

Ellie laughed. He was referring to the time they'd made love under the apple tree, her suggestion one night because of the full moon, and how she froze her butt off, teeth chattering, and…. "Well, that was rather good," she'd said afterwards, both scrambling to get back into their clothes.

"And don't say it's because I remind you of Damian either."

Ellie smiled. He did, dark hair, strong neck and back, well-defined muscles…same spirit, same kindness in their eyes at times, same deadliness at others. "It's because you're honest."

Diablo leaned close and kissed her. "About being a good lover?"

"Yes," Ellie nodded, touching him. "And about who you are."

"Which is…?"

"A man standing on his own two feet."

Diablo glanced away and shrugged. "Is there any other way?"

"For you? No." Ellie watched him pick up a stone and toss it in the air. There were bats overhead. One flew down to investigate and took to the sky again. "And because you *are* a good lover."

Diablo looked at her with a promise in his smile. The two finished their ice cream in silence as the bats soared above.

~ 8 ~

Ellie's day job was at the Whitright Desktop Publishing Firm where she worked as a typesetter. And it was just that, a job. Ellie admittedly was not a career person. She worked strictly for the paycheck, and didn't care about the challenge, or the glory. Even when her boss praised her for "a job well done," something the woman did often, it meant very little. Ellie would smile and thank her for the compliment, and that's as much thought as it elicited. Ellie liked her boss; they got along well. She might even be a friend, had Ellie met her elsewhere. But as it was, all the woman ever talked about was work, and so....

Ellie glanced at the clock. She'd promised to bring Grandma Betty her old patchwork-quilt on the way to the laundromat, but wanted to swing by the barn first.

"I'm thinking I should have it here when I die," Grandma Betty had said, "so you can make sure it goes with me. Okay?"

Ellie nodded. "Did you make the quilt, Grandma?"

"No, not that I recall. I think I bought it at a garage sale or something."

Ellie smiled. "How long have you had it?"

Grandma Betty couldn't recall that either. "Oh...a long time, I think."

Ellie stopped by her apartment and picked up the quilt. It had been months now since Grandma Betty sent it home with her. "Wash it and just keep it there till winter," she'd said. "I'm tired of getting pee all over it." About that time she'd developed a bladder infection and had become incontinent. Initially, there was the hope that this was a temporary condition. It wasn't.

Ellie had two letters waiting for her at home. One was from a feminist organization soliciting funds for a facility to house "Women in Transition." And the other, a disconnection notice on her phone. She got one every month, and always paid it within the allotted time, but could never seem to get ahead. She tossed them both on the table, and headed for the barn. It was a quick stop, nothing amiss in the stall, and Damian's hip seemed to be all but healed.

Grandma Betty was happy to see her earlier than expected. "You won't believe what just happened," she said.

Ellie sat down next to her.

"I had a dream."

Ellie smiled. "In the daytime?"

"Yep. As God is my witness."

Ellie laughed. Grandma Betty didn't believe in God. Not in the traditional sense at least. Ellie adjusted Grandma Betty's pillow. She looked so tiny, so frail. "What kind of dream?"

"One of the sand ones."

"With the hour glass?"

"Yes. Only the sand was all different colors, like the sculptures, and you should've seen how everything turned out. It was awful! Blue where it shouldn't have been. A whole bunch of white in one spot. And the red, I couldn't even see the red anymore. How can a color just disappear?"

"I don't know." They'd had these kinds of discussions before.

"Do you think I should get my hair done?"

Ellie stared for a moment, then caught on. It had been months since Grandma Betty had her hair colored, maybe it was time.

"I didn't think it mattered, what with my dying soon and all. But maybe it does. And you know what else? They're threatening to kick old man Smith out. Said he won't stop playing with his louie."

Ellie laughed, but even so, blushed.

"I say let the old man be. Hang a do-not-disturb sign on his door and let him go to town!"

Ellie laughed again. "Do you want me to go see if the beautician has time tomorrow?"

"I don't know. How faded am I?"

Grandma Betty loved the color red! Red cars, red lipstick, red fingernails, red hair.

"I think you're due."

"How much do they charge again?"

"Not that much. Don't worry about it."

* * *

Ellie phoned her father and was promptly put on hold. She hated asking him for money, but what else could she do? "It's for Grandma's hair," she said, and was on hold again before she got a reply. She glanced at the clock on the stove in her kitchen. Abby was due any minute.

"How much did you say?"

"Forty dollars."

"Okay, I'll get it in the mail. How you doin'?"

"Good." She heard Abby outside the door. "I'll talk to you later. Give Mom my love, I gotta go."

Ellie's mom was actually her stepmother. She never really knew her birth mother; she'd died in a one-car automobile accident when Ellie was only ten months old and still nursing. Fortunately Ellie couldn't remember that time in her life, or the colic and dysentery she suffered for weeks following her mother's death. She did, however, remember her father marrying Jewel, even though it was just a little over a year later and Ellie still a toddler. She even remembered what Jewel was wearing that day. Seafoam green. From head to toe. Seafoam green. It was the first time she'd ever heard the word seafoam, and heard it over and over that whole day.

Abby was all excited. She and Ellie were going to a summer solstice celebration, her first one, and she could hardly wait. "Do you think we'll howl at the moon or something?"

Ellie laughed. "You can howl if you like." Diablo had pulled another graveyard shift for the night, so Ellie wasn't feeling guilty for a change, and said she just might howl herself. At first he'd told her he wasn't working and pretended to sulk, then finally that he was, and Ellie asked why the pretense.

"To keep you on your toes," he'd said.

"I don't need to be kept on my toes," Ellie responded, pushing him away.

"Oh but you do," he insisted

Abby had bought them both Native American beaded headbands, which she declared essential to wear, along with tied-dyed T-shirts and faded jeans, and had made crystal medallions that hung on chains for around their necks. Ellie joked that they were overdressed, but they weren't. Not unless you counted the fact that they were the only ones wearing shoes.

Lolita was nowhere to be seen. Ellie hadn't seen her for hours, let alone the flock, but thought nothing of it. This time of year, it was not unusual for them to disappear for hours, sometimes days on end.

"Oh, look," Abby said. Across the way sat the flower-child woman, who gazed up from her knitting and smiled. Abby waved. "Wonder what she's doing here?"

Ellie shrugged.

Most of the women assembled, they knew. All were on the same path of sorts and always bumping into one another here and there at these retreats. Some had their daughters and little nieces with them. It was a small group. Abby counted twenty-two attendees, including the children. One little girl had medieval-looking braces on her legs.

The ceremony began with a series of readings.

Brush Fire.
Fallen timbers, the grass smolders.
Bronze leaves, now charcoal gray.
An eerie silence, a smoky stench.
Clouds now come, much too late.

Abby looked at Ellie. "What's that mean?"

"I don't know," Ellie whispered.

"It sounds defeatist."

Ellie smiled. That, or realistic.

Creativity has no place in contentment. Awareness is the vaccine that eradicates the terminal disease.

Abby stared. Ellie stared. The flower-child woman stared. "A light refreshment will now be served."

"Thank goodness," Abby said. "I was starting to get depressed."

Clouds, in the shapes of elephants and gazelles soared overhead as a tall thin woman sat down next to them at a table, dressed from head to toe in "all things natural and handmade."

"See, look here. Even my bra," she said, turning around and raising her shirt for them to see the label. "Hand picked, hand woven, 100% cotton."

"Wow," Abby said, noting the size. "Must have been one hell of a plant."

"No insecticides, no dyes, nothing," the woman said proudly. "It's all organic. I am in complete harmony with nature."

"Cool."

"Even my shoes, natural cowhide."

"As opposed to...?" Ellie said.

Abby gave her a look; this as the woman fished out a pair of shoes from her hemp bag for them to inspect up close. "Guess how much I paid for them. Go ahead, guess."

Abby examined them carefully. "$59.95."

The woman's mouth dropped. "Not hardly, they're genuine moccasins. Guess again."

It was Ellie's turn. "Uh.... How did they get them red?"

"Oh, I'm so glad you asked. They soak them in beet juice. Isn't that awesome?"

"Yep." Both Ellie and Abby agreed it was awesome, and next came an all natural "water bladder."

"Natural how?" Abby asked, tucking her arms to her sides. The woman handed it to Ellie.

"It holds a full liter and guaranteed to stay cold for six hours."

Ellie handed it back. "That's nice. Why's it empty?"

"I forgot to fill it," the woman said, without missing a beat. "And last but not least...." She dug down and produced a tiny drawstring satchel from deep inside her bag. "Freeze-dried Peyote."

"Oh shit," Ellie said, and started to laugh.

*   *   *

Nightfall brought an air of seriousness. A somberness. And another reading.

The lady I love is where I live.
She now has nothing more to give.

Then a dance, a sacred dance; the reason for the flower-child woman's presence. A dance that with every move, every expression, exhibited joy and evoked heartbreak. A celebration, a mourning. Laughter and tears. Conception and birth. And in the end, as she raised her eyes and beseeched the moon, a collective pause.

Ellie glanced away.

"As we look to the North, to the South, to the East, and to the West, we celebrate the body of the earth. The feminine, the yin. Fertility, sovereignty, and sustenance. We beseech life. We beseech death."

Death indeed. Here came the mosquitoes, which posed a dilemma. To spray, or not to spray? Kill or repel? Annihilate or ignore. For a moment, it seemed a helpless situation, all the women swatting themselves and feeling guilty. But the situation was promptly remedied. The organizers announced they had everything under control, and had just simply forgotten to put out their arsenal of citronella candles, which were passed around then and quickly lighted. Abby thought it added to the atmosphere, particularly since the citronella didn't necessarily work its best at first and so everyone drew closer to the campfire as they devised an impenetrable stand of candles around them.

Ellie and Abby were hunkered down between a mother and a daughter, who were by all appearances, "on the outs." Abby introduced them. "This is Olivia and this is Erica. Erica's in seventh grade, wants a nose-ring, and got two "F's" on her last report card."

Ellie glanced from one to the other, and shook her head in wonder. Abby was a marvel.

"Olivia is a psychologist."

Ellie smiled supportively at little Erica.

Trays carrying frosted wine glasses brimming with a frothy strawberry beverage were circulated that proved sweet, yet tart, with an aftertaste of lemon to symbolize fertility and ultimate labor.

Thanks was given to the birth of the season, to all seasons, to the everlasting sun and the infinite moon. And to the night, this very night, "When light reaches the limit of its power over darkness. We give thanks to the goddess above. To the goddess within. And to the circle of life. The energy of life. Life itself."

"This is awesome," Abby whispered.

Ellie nodded, unsure if she meant the juice, or the night. Or both.

"As the spear is to the male, so the cauldron is to the female." The flower-child woman threw something into the fire that hissed. "For you, Earth Mother. Blessed be."

~ 9 ~

Grandma Betty talked of having no regrets, but did have some. She stared at the ceiling, counting them to herself. There was the time she jumped out of a moving car and then lied about it and said she was pushed. And there was that day....

"Betty?"

"Yes?" Grandma Betty turned, startled somewhat, and looked at the aide standing next to her bed.

"What do you need?"

"Who me? I don't know," she said. "A new body, I guess." She laughed at her own joke.

The aide laughed, too. "Is that what you rang for?"

Grandma Betty puzzled and glanced at her hand. Apparently she'd pressed the light button. It was right at her fingertips. "Well, I'll be damned. How's come when I don't happen to need anything, you come right away?"

The aide laughed again, then adjusted Grandma Betty's blanket and fluffed her pretty red hair. "What're you all dolled up for, Betty?"

"Nothing," Grandma Betty said. "Absolutely nothing." The way she figured it, she had days before she'd get around to dying. And she wasn't expecting any company until tomorrow, unless you counted the church lady who came every Thursday. "What's her name?"

"Who?"

Grandma Betty frowned. "That woman from the church. The one that comes and prays all the time."

"Oh, her. I think her name's Deborah."

"Deborah? Really. Now that's a nice name." She'd gone to school with a Deborah. Deborah Watson, a plain girl with a big forehead, if she recalled correctly.

"Can I get you something, Betty? Something out of your fridge?"

"Oh...." Grandma Betty thought for a minute. Starving herself was getting harder and harder. At times it was tempting to eat. "See if I have any of them puddings left."

The aide checked her refrigerator and turned. "Vanilla or chocolate?"

Grandma Betty hesitated. "Never mind. You go ahead and have one. Take whichever you like."

The woman took a chocolate one, thanked her and left, and Grandma Betty found herself staring at the ceiling again. Now where was I? Oh yes, regrets. She folded her arms across her chest. I shouldn't have lied about being pushed out of that car. It got a lot of people in trouble. And I was to blame for that potato salad spoiling that one day, too. I honestly thought it would be okay, but so many people got the runs later. She looked around. "I wonder if I should be writing this stuff down."

* * *

Ellie and Abby peered into the Teepee set up for the occasion, and backed out quickly. "All natural lady" was inside, showing off her moccasins and she'd already cornered them twice tonight. "God, what is it with that woman and those friggin' shoes?" Abby said. "If she shows them to me one more time, I swear I'm gonna smack her upside the head with them!"

Ellie chuckled. It was still "mingling time," time set aside to get to know one another. "To open and to share, and to allow others into your space and touch your soul before the ultimate hour of silence and solitude."

"Quick! Here she comes!" Abby whispered. They made their way across the lawn and close to the campfire, which had become more and more of a bonfire. Several women danced around its perimeter, one humming while the other swayed and bowed, and chanted in what sounded like a Native American tongue.

"I've been meaning to tell you," Abby said, when they found a place to sit. "People at the barn are talking about you."

"Me?" Ellie looked at her. "Why?"

Abby shrugged. "I don't know. Because of Victor, I guess."

"Why? What's he saying?"

"It's not so much what he's saying, as what he's doing."

"Which is…?"

Abby hesitated. The little girl with leg braces was walking painfully toward them. "He's building a bird cage. A really large one from what I understand."

Ellie bowed her head and stared at the ground. She could see Lolita confined, frantic and beating her wings against the bars. When she raised her eyes, the little girl was standing directly in front of them.

"Hello," Abby said. "This is Ellie, and I'm Abby. What's your name?"

"Andrea," the little girl said, balancing herself. "Poor little Andrea."

"Oh!" Abby smiled. "Well in that case, I'm acne Abby and this is uh…weird Ellie."

Ellie laughed. For Abby's sake. For the little girl's sake. For her own sake. The little girl giggled, handed them a pamphlet, and went on with her arduous task of passing them out.

Ellie watched her. "That's so sad. I wonder what's wrong with her legs."

"Polio," Abby said. "Her mom doesn't believe in modern medicine."

Ellie looked at Abby.

"I heard it from someone earlier who knows her really well. The mom I mean."

Ellie stared at the little girl. "I wonder how the mother justifies this."

Abby shook her head. "I don't know. But look at her. She looks wise beyond her years. Do you think she's an old soul?"

Ellie shrugged. "Could be."

"I wish I was an old soul."

"Why? What would you be doing different?"

Abby smiled. "Well for one, I probably wouldn't be dragging you to all these retreats."

"You mean I'd have to go alone."

Abby shook her head and grew very serious. "Come on, Ellie. I know you only come because of me. And I want you to know I appreciate it. I couldn't come alone. I just...." Abby bit at her bottom lip, her chin beginning to quiver, and glanced away.

"What? What's the matter?"

"Nothing," Abby said. "I just want you to know I appreciate it."

"All right, so I know." Ellie said. "Sheesh, it's nothing to cry about. Come on." She nudged Abby playfully and Abby wiped her eyes and laughed.

"What *am* I searching for? What am I hoping to find?"

Ellie shrugged. "I don't know. But at the moment, we're in for silence and solitude."

"What?"

Ellie motioned to the almost visible wave of quiet making its way toward them, a hush but for the crackle and whirl of the fire. Abby glanced at her watch. It was time.

*   *   *

Grandma Betty had one final regret. The one she always had; dying in a nursing home. She could see herself now, just like in the stories she'd read or seen on TV. There she'd be, hovering around the ceiling and looking down at her lifeless body just laying there, all pasty and thin, a damned diaper on...probably soiled to beat the band, her mouth hung open. She shivered. No, not her. She was going to die with her mouth closed and that's all there was to it. And since she'd quit eating, how bad could her diaper be?

She sighed. It won't be long now, she thought, and really wished she could remember dying previously so she'd know what to expect. She hoped it didn't hurt too much. She hated pain. Not that she ever thought of herself as particularly weak or fragile. She never used to be at least. But lately, the last couple of months, pain, even the slightest pain, was practically unbearable. Why didn't the nurses understand? "When I tell them I'm in pain, I'm in pain. I hurt all over sometimes. Last night it was my head, and tonight it's my legs. But we just gave you something, Betty, they'll say. You've had enough. Enough of what I should ask, pain?"

She glanced at the curtain between the beds, and wondered who was on the other side. For a long time it was Margaret, then that woman April. "Thirty days hath September, April, June and November. All the rest have thirty-one, except...."

"Betty?"

"Yes?" She looked around, in a different room, a different hour.

"Do you know your ABC's?"

"Yes."

"Do you want to recite them?"

"No. And I don't want to play with these goddamned blocks either! I'm not a child! Why are you treating me like a child? I hate it here! I hate it!"

"I'm sorry, Betty. But you must keep your mind active."

"What? By saying the ABC's? That's active? That's nothing! I'm not doing it! April? April, are you asleep?" Of course she is, Betty thought. She always is. That woman could sleep 24 hours a day, and talk about stink....

"We're going to have to call your son."

"My son? Why?"

"Because you're not cooperating. You've been assigned occupational and physical therapy, and you're not even trying, Betty."

"Go ahead and call him. No, don't! I'll try. Give me the blocks."

"Fine, Betty. But if you throw them again...."

"I won't," she promised, and sent them flying.

"A, b, c, d, e, f, g...." She sang at the top of her lungs.

*   *   *

At first, silence and solitude was nice. Space, allow yourself space, they were instructed. Ellie liked space. Abby did not. She kept looking at Ellie and making funny faces.

"Find the voice within yourself. Calm the voice within yourself."

Abby sighed. The voice inside her wouldn't shut up. It was screaming bloody murder. "How far can you see?" she whispered to Ellie.

"What?"

"How far can you see?"

Ellie shrugged, hoping to appease her. But Abby persisted, pointing straight ahead, past the fire, past the circle of women, past the Teepee. "How far?"

"To the oak tree," Ellie whispered.

Abby stared. She didn't see an oak tree. She didn't see any trees. "How far is that?"

"I don't know," Ellie whispered. They were on a slight knoll. "A mile, maybe two. Why?"

"Because I just realized something. I don't see well in the dark."

"So...."

"Shhhhhh...."

"So, I think I just had a vision."

Ellie stared, waited for her to crack a smile, laugh, giggle, something. Nothing. "What kind of vision?"

"I don't know. Flashes of lights and things."

"It's the fire."

"Shhhhhhh!!!!!"

"No, it's not. Honest." She edged closer to Ellie and crossed the invisible line of space. "I think we should leave."

"Why?"

"Because I'm scared."

"Of what?"

"I don't know. Let's go."

They left.

~ 10 ~

There was a message from the administrator waiting for Ellie when she arrived at the nursing home. "An urgent matter," it read. "Come see me right away." Ellie looked in on Grandma Betty first; she was sleeping, and headed for the office. A nurse, in passing, scowled at her.

She knocked on the administrator's door and was told to come in. "Have a seat, please."

Ellie sat down warily. Even though the woman had smiled when offering her a seat, there was something in her eyes.

"Are you aware that your grandmother is attempting to starve herself to death?"

"Yes."

"I see." The woman sat back, nodding. "We were afraid that was the case."

Ellie just looked at her.

"It is against Mission Grove's policy to allow death by malnutrition, which I'm sure you are aware of, and even though at this stage of life, it can be an extreme burden to a resident's family and tempting to not want to prolong life...."

"Wait a minute," Ellie said. "What are you saying?"

The woman hesitated. "I'm saying, that even though I can understand how busy a person's life is, and how coming to a nursing home on a regular basis...."

Ellie sat stunned, appalled. "Grandma Betty is the one that wants to die. It's not my decision. She's says it's her time."

"Yes. But, surely you realize she's not thinking straight. That being ill has...."

"No," Ellie said. "I do not realize that. My Grandma Betty is thinking perfectly clear. She's tired. She's tired of being sick, she's tired of being in pain, and she just plain doesn't want to live any longer."

The woman studied her. "And you're tired, too. I can see that. That's why dealing with situations such as this are best left to professionals. Someone not so close to the situation."

Ellie shook her head. "She hates it here. You have to know that."

"Yes, but we also know that she has nowhere else to go. I've spoken with your father...."

Ellie stared.

"And as her POA, he is in full agreement. Either she eats or we're looking at a stomach tube. I've taken the liberty to check on her insurances...." When the woman started shuffling through some papers, Ellie stood to leave. Whenever the mention of her father or Medicaid was brought up, she knew better than to argue. "Might I ask you a question?" she ventured from the door.

"Yes."

"Are there other nursing homes that don't have this policy? Ones that would allow her, her wish to die?"

"Yes," the woman said. "But trust me, I don't think you'd want her there."

Ellie felt the impact of that statement wash over her. "Does my grandmother know?"

"Yes, I talked to her just a little while ago. Obviously she's upset, but that's just the way it is. And if I might give you some advice. You seem like a nice young woman and I've been told you are very attentive to your grandmother. I'm sure you want what's best for her. But you can't think like a child in this matter, a grandchild, if you will. You have to be the adult now, and the bottom line is, this is not your grandmother's decision."

* * *

Diablo listened somewhat sympathetically to Ellie's account of the conversation, but seemed more concerned with the hockey game on her TV.

"I wonder if it's a law," Ellie said, thinking out loud.

"Probably."

Ellie looked at him; studied his profile, the angle of his nose, his jaw line. "You agree with them, don't you?"

Diablo shrugged.

Ellie leaned her head back and stared at the ceiling. "Why does everything have to be so difficult? Why can't just one thing be easy? Why can't we just die when we want to?"

Diablo glanced at her and with another glance, turned off the TV. "Look. I can't even believe you want your grandmother to die. You talk about it like it's nothing. You say you love her and yet...."

Ellie held up her hands. "I *don't want* my grandmother to die. I wish you all would stop saying that. It's she who wants to die. It's her time, Diablo. If she lived in the wild...." She trailed off.

"The wild? Like up in Alaska, dinner for the wolves."

Ellie sighed. "You don't understand."

"You got that right."

Ellie paused and shook her head. "No, but you think nothing of getting mad almost every day when I go see her."

"What, so you're saying this is all my fault? That you're wanting her to die because of me?"

Ellie looked at him, just looked at him for a moment. "You know, I never realized just how selfish you are until now. This isn't about you. And it isn't about me."

Diablo sat back, that all too familiar anger flickering in his eyes.

"You amaze me. There you sit, passing judgment on me, when all I want for my Grandma is what she wants. And yet, if you had *your* way, I'd go see her once a week, if that."

"That's not true."

"Yeah, right. I'll bet you can't even remember the last time you saw your own grandmother, let alone care about mine. So please...spare me, okay."

"Fine. Consider yourself spared," he said. He grabbed his keys and went home.

*   *   *

Abby waited and waited, then went ahead and tacked Bubba and started riding, assuming Ellie would arrive shortly. She'd probably get after her about her riding alone.

"You don't ride alone, just like you don't swim alone." But after all, Ellie always rode alone. Why shouldn't she?

Ellie found her on the ground and in tears. "Are you all right?"

"No." She just sat there, dirt all over her, even in her hair.

"What happened?"

"I don't know."

Bubba was at the far end of the arena, reins down over his head and nosing around in the sawdust.

"Come on, let's get you up." Ellie pulled Abby to her feet, helped dust her off, and jokingly asked if she could move her arms and legs. It was obvious she could. Bubba needed more attention at the moment. If he took another step forward, chances are he'd get hung up on a rein. "Where's your helmet?"

"Uh...."

While Abby went for her helmet, Ellie retrieved Bubba and started back across the arena. "Are you sure you're all right? Nothing broken?"

Abby shook her head. She was older than Ellie and towered over her, but at times, like now, Abby reminded her of a child.

"I can't believe he dumped me like that. Why'd he do that?"

Ellie shrugged, checking his tack. "I don't know. He's a horse. Horses do strange things sometimes. Just like some people I happen to know," she added, hoping to make Abby laugh, to lighten the situation. It had the opposite effect.

"Do you think he'll do it again?"

Ellie smiled. "I doubt it. Since you don't exactly recall how you landed on your butt in the first place, it would be pretty hard to duplicate."

That succeeded in making Abby laugh, but then all too quickly, she turned grave again. This wasn't the first time she'd been thrown, and if not thrown, fallen. "We were just cantering along and the next thing I knew, I was on the ground."

Ellie looked at her. "Oh, I hate when that happens."

Abby laughed again. She'd never seen Ellie get dumped. She'd never even seen her come close to getting dumped. "I'll never learn to ride. Not like you, at least."

"Sure you will. Now come up. Up you go."

Abby hesitated. "Maybe there's something wrong with him. Do you think he has something wrong with him?"

"No. Nothing a little exercise won't cure."

Abby sighed and mounted, felt around for her stirrups, as she'd been taught, no looking, and then just sat there. "What should I do?"

Ellie glanced up at her. "Whatever you want. Just don't fall again till I come back out. Okay?"

Abby smiled. What would she do without Ellie? She always had a way of cheering her up and making her feel better. Even with the vision that night at the solstice party, the premonition, frightening as it was, all those dancing and falling lights, danger lurking somewhere. "I swear, Ellie. One of us is going to die. I know that's what it meant."

"We're all going to die," Ellie had said, "sooner or later. So unless your vision registered a prescribed date and time...."

Lolita cawed from a tree branch outside the window. Once, twice, three times. Far off in the distance, a mocking bird sang a taunting song. Abby walked Bubba around the perimeter of the arena, round and round, and was relieved when Ellie finally appeared with Damian. Bubba was always happier with another horse in the ring. "Did you ride yesterday?"

"No." Ellie adjusted Damian's girth up one notch and then another. "I had to meet with the undertaker."

"Honestly?"

Ellie nodded and motioned. "Remember, seeing eyes. No running up on us."

Abby chuckled. She had a habit of concentrating so hard on one particular aspect of riding, she would sometimes lose sight of where she was in the arena in respect to other horses, and would ride up practically right on top of them. That, or cut them off coming the other way, since she was also prone to reversing directions without telling the other riders, and....

It was precisely that latter move which sparked their friendship. Ellie yelled, "Heads up!" one fine Saturday morning. Abby attributed it to saving her life. And they'd been buddies ever since.

Damian was feeling his oats and "on the muscle" from the get-go, dancing and prancing and tossing his head. "I probably should have lunged him first," Ellie commented, when he'd taken to cantering in place, trying to pull the reins out of her hands.

Abby marveled. Ellie never got rattled, never got angry. Firm, yes, she'd seen Ellie get after Damian, but never harshly. Her method of bringing him down was to "trot the hell out of him." Along the wall, down the sides, small circles, large circles, across the diagonal, more circles, and all the while she talked to him. Eventually Damian started to relax on the bit. And it was then, as Abby was trotting at the other end of the arena, that Bubba suddenly dropped his shoulder, bolted to the inside, and dumped her again.

She landed hard on her back. Ellie thought she heard something snap from way over where she was riding, but couldn't get to her right away. Bubba began running around the arena, snorting, his stirrup leathers and stirrups slapping against his sides. That was all Damian needed to start acting up again. He commenced to bucking and dancing and propping and wheeling - and then he bucked some more. It took some time for Ellie to get him in hand and calmed down enough to try and dismount.

Meanwhile, Abby just lay there.

* * *

Grandma Betty insisted she be allowed to walk to the bathroom on her own, even though it had been months since she'd even stood unassisted. "Your legs are too weak, Betty. You'll fall. Here, let us help you." The two aides positioned Grandma Betty's walker in front of her and gently helped her rise to her feet, where she teetered and wobbled for a moment on toothpick-like legs, and ultimately plopped back down in her chair.

She felt an agonizing pain inside, deep inside, that reminded her of childbirth. "Oh, that hurts," she moaned.

"Where, Betty?" one of the aides asked.

"In my womb."

"Your womb?" The two women looked at one another and tried not to laugh, but did not succeed. "Oh Betty, I don't think you even have a womb anymore."

Grandma Betty got mad. "Yes I do!" she insisted. "I had children."

"Yeah, but I think you also had a hysterectomy. I think I read it on your chart."

Grandma Betty looked up at the woman. "You're a nosy little bitch, you know that?"

The young woman laughed. "Probably so, but I want to know everything there is about my favorite residents, so I took a look. You had a complete hysterectomy in your forties and two fourteen-pound tumors removed at the same time."

Grandma Betty shook her head in disgust. "A lot you know. Just the one weighed fourteen pounds. The second one only weighed five."

The aide smiled. "Even so, no womb. Now tell me again, where are you feeling pain?"

"Nowhere," Grandma Betty said, and laughed suddenly. "I'm feeling no pain." Saying that reminded her of the good old days at the American Legion. How the men, veterans, all of them, brave men, would get drunk and say they were "feeling no pain." And how the one time Bill fell off the barstool and banged his chin on the bar, and.... One of the aides started out the room to answer a call.

"Wait. Come help me get Betty into bed first. Betty, are you ready to go to bed?"

Grandma Betty nodded.

"Okay, fine. But you know you need to say please, right?"

Grandma Betty looked up at her, focused on her eyes. "Yes. Would you put me to bed now, please?"

The aide nodded her approval. "That's a good girl. Yes, I will." The two women went about their task of undressing and washing Grandma Betty, changing her diaper, powdering her, and getting her into her nightgown. The one has such gentle hands, thought Betty, as they lifted her into bed and straightened her around. And the other, the one who insisted she always say please and thank you for every little thing, she had a pepperminty scent.

"Thank you," Grandma Betty remembered to say repeatedly throughout. "Thank you. Thank you. Thank you."

* * *

"Abby...? Abby?" Ellie leaned over her. "Abby, are you okay?"

Abby opened her eyes and stared. "I don't know. I think so. What'd I do? Fall again?"

"Yes. Do you want me to go get help?"

"No," Abby said, "just let me lay here a second."

Ellie glanced over her shoulder at Damian and Bubba, both tied to the arena gate and fervently trying to reach one another by pawing their way.

"Ellie!" they heard someone yell. "Ellie, you gonna ride?"

"Oh, shit," Abby said. "Quick, it's Julie. Help me get up."

Before Ellie could even blink, Abby was upright, and in the next instant on her feet. For the second time that day, Ellie helped dust her off.

"Don't say anything, okay?"

Ellie nodded, watching with great concern as Abby put her helmet back on and staggered toward Bubba.

"Ellie?" The little girl called out again, "Ellie, where are you?" She'd obviously just looked for her in the tack room and from the sound of her voice was headed around the corner in their direction. "Oh, there you are. Can you guys stay till I ride?"

Ellie answered for both with a quick nod and another glance at Abby, who was halfway across the arena. She caught up with her and kept her voice low. "Are you sure you're okay? You fell really hard." She didn't want to mention that snap she heard, but it was utmost on her mind, to say the least.

"I'm fine. You know what they always say, you included, about falling and getting right back on."

"Yes, I know, but...."

Abby marched right up between Damian and Bubba, untied Bubba, and pulled the reins over his head. She hesitated only a second before mounting. Ellie didn't know if it was from apprehension or pain, but up she went, and Ellie quickly untied Damian and mounted also.

"Walk beside me for awhile. Okay?"

Ellie nodded.

* * *

Grandma Betty had the worst night of her life. She dreamt she gave birth to a litter of chipmunks. And when she woke, the pad underneath her was full of blood.

"Well, isn't that wonderful!" she told the day nurse, who seemed very concerned. "My favorite color, red!"

"This isn't funny, Betty. This is serious."

"Obviously," Grandma Betty said, judging from the look on her face

"Just when we got you eating again, now this! I hope you're happy."

Grandma Betty drew a ragged breath. "Does this mean my time is near?"

The nurse hesitated. Besides the blood, there was the conspicuous absence of urine. "Probably, yes."

"Then I'm happy," Grandma Betty said.

Ellie got a phone call at work just before noon, and was surprised to hear her grandmother's frail little voice on the other end of the line. "It's happening, Ellie," she said. "They say I'm dying."

Silence. Ellie had prepared herself for this moment, for this day. It was the inevitable they'd been waiting for, hoping for. Still, she had to steady herself, to sit down, to stop the room from spinning, and collect her thoughts. What to do? What to say? "I'm so excited for you, Grandma. I really am." She could hear herself saying it, she may even have said it twice, then promised she'd come right over, and hung up the phone.

Her boss looked up from her desk across the room. "Is everything okay?"

"No, um...." She reached for her purse. "It's my grandmother. She's dying, and I need to be there."

"Oh, but of course," the woman said, and came around to see what Ellie had been working on. "Take all the time you need."

Ellie thanked her, left, and in the lobby, stopped to phone her father. "It's Grandma, she just called, and...."

"Yes, I know. She phoned here, too. I don't know what she expects me to do. I can't just drop everything. I've got three contracts that have to be signed today, one I was just about to hop on a plane to seal, and...."

"Okay, I'll tell her."

"Good. Tell her I'll try to get there later today, say six o'clock or so, or early in the morning."

"Dad, did you talk to her?"

"No, I talked to the nurse."

* * *

Ellie rounded the hallway by the nurses' station, which was empty, and expected to see every nurse from the floor gathered in her grandmother's room. There wasn't a one. Just Grandma Betty, all bundled up in bed in her patchwork-quilt.

"Oh, Ellie," she said. "I'm so glad you're here. Turn my TV on. I don't know what they did with my remote."

Ellie smiled. Leave it to Grandma Betty to want to watch her soaps the day she was dying. Ellie turned the set on and found the right channel.

"Turn it down a little, dear. I need to talk to you about a plan."

"A plan?"

Grandma Betty lowered her voice. "I'm telling everyone I have a dying wish to see the old neighborhood one more time."

"And...?"

"And, you're not going to bring me back. When I die, you can just take me to the undertaker's."

Ellie found herself smiling again. On the way over, she had no idea what to expect and feared one look at Grandma Betty near death and she'd be reduced to tears. Not so. Not with her grandmother in such good spirits.

"The way I figure it, I'll probably die during the night or very early in the morning. So, after we leave, I'll never have to come back."

"But where will we go?" Her grandmother didn't really have an old neighborhood. In her own words, she "moved around a lot."

"Well, I'd like to ride by the Legion one more time. And I'd like to go to the cemetery."

"The cemetery?" Why the cemetery?

"And I'd like to go to the...."

A nurse entered the room. "I understand you're taking Betty for a ride this afternoon to see her old house."

Ellie nodded.

"How long do you think this will take?"

Ellie shrugged, unsure of what to say, unsure of anything, everything. How was she going to get her grandmother into the car, and then out? Was this the right thing to do? Did she have enough gas in the car? "Not long, I guess."

"How far away? I just looked at your chart, Betty, and it says you used to live on the West Side. Is that where you'll be going?"

Grandma Betty nodded. "Why? What's the big deal?"

The nurse sighed. "Your meds, Betty. You'll be due again at o-nineteen hundred."

"So, I can tell time. Give them to me and I'll take them myself if I'm not back by then."

"Sorry, that's not allowed." The nurse reached instinctively to check Grandma Betty's pulse. It was beating quite strong. She felt her forehead, no fever yet. "I suggest you go right after the dinner hour."

"Why? You're not still going to make me try and eat, are you?"

The nurse glanced at them both and shook her head. She uncovered Grandma Betty's legs and removed both socks to examine her feet. "It would just work out better that way."

Grandma Betty turned to Ellie. "What do you think? Is that all right?"

Ellie stared. "Dad said he'd try and get here around six."

"Good," Grandma Betty said. "That's perfect. We'll leave right after that then. Okay?"

"Okay." With the nurse standing there and not knowing the rest of the plan, what else *could* Ellie say?

~ 11 ~

Mid-afternoon, Grandma Betty sent Ellie away. "I mean it. Go. Come back later." Ellie could see her slipping further and further before her very eyes.

"Why don't I just stay?"

"Because," Grandma Betty said. "I'm sure you have other things to do. Besides, I want to take a nap so I can dream one more time. I'm going to miss dreaming. Now go."

Feeling lost, Ellie headed for the barn. There was no reason to return to work; work seemed meaningless at the moment. She stopped by Abby's house to see if she wanted to join her.

"Yes, but not to ride. I'm never riding again. I quit."

"What? Why?" The sound that Ellie had heard snap the other day, was apparently Abby's spirit.

"I'm sick of falling. I can't ride for shit anyway, so what's the use?"

Ellie sighed. Surely there was something she could say, something encouraging, something…. She couldn't come up with anything, her mind reeling with thoughts of Grandma Betty and her last day on earth.

"I think I'm going to sell Bubba anyway."

"What?" Ellie looked at her. "Come on. No, you're not."

"Yes, I am. He deserves a better rider, a better owner. I suck."

Ellie shook her head. "You'd better not let him hear you say that. You know how gullible he is. He just might believe you. And then what?"

Abby smiled a half-hearted smile, bolstered for a second. It only took a little coaxing after that, to convince her to come along. By the time they arrived, it had started to rain. Victor was working on his birdcage. "I hate that man," Ellie said. And the way she'd said it, first, the glance in his direction, then a sudden stiffness in her posture, stopped Abby in her wake.

"Wow! You know you looked just like Lolita right then."

Ellie shrugged. "I am Lolita. She's a part of me; I'm a part of her."

"Exactly." Abby marveled. "I can see it. Which reminds me, I saw a flyer for this organization the other day that was all about crows. I found it at the health food store of all places. There was a picture of a crow on it, which caught my eye, and it talked all about how crows work together for the common good. And get this; it also said that in the mythology of a number of cultures, the crow is revered as the messenger and the healer. Isn't that awesome? I remember thinking, cool, I wonder if that woman we met at the retreat knew about that stuff, with the way she acted about Lolita getting stung and what she said about you being alone and all."

Ellie smiled, recalling the woman's expression. "I wouldn't be surprised."

"Have the crows been with you all your life?"

"For the most part," Ellie said. There were times, particularly in her mid-teens, when they were way far in the distance. She'd chased them away. She'd wanted to fit in then, and couldn't exactly do that with a flock of crows following her around. She told people she'd stopped feeding them, and they believed her. Even Jewel believed her.

"I want a crow of my own," Abby declared. "Do you think one of the flock would adopt me?"

"I don't know. I think they would have done it by now." Ellie could never remember a day when she didn't feel an affinity for the crows, a connection. "You might not be a crow."

"What am I then?"

Ellie reached for her saddle and bridle and looked at her. "Are you still a vegetarian?"

"Sort of. Why? What's that mean?"

"I'm not sure. I'm just guessing. I think you're probably a parrot, since you do like to make a fuss and talk a lot."

Abby laughed. When she was nervous, like now, she did tend to rattle on.

"Then again, you could be a parakeet. You're also very domesticated."

"So what are you saying? Do you think maybe I should go out and buy one?"

Ellie chuckled. "Yeah, right. I can see Victor now, with you riding around with a parakeet perched on your shoulder. Wouldn't that go over big?"

Abby grabbed her tack and followed along. Bubba and Damian both nickered at the sounds of their voices. One look in Bubba's stall at all 1200 pounds of him and Abby's stomach started doing flip-flops. "What if he dumps me again?"

"What if he doesn't? Then what?"

Abby stared. Good point. One she'd cling to. "What's Victor's thing with the crows anyway? It's not like they come close. And it's not like every horse in the barn isn't vaccinated against West Nile."

Ellie put Damian's halter and shank on him, gave him a big hug, and led him to one set of the crossties to groom and tack him. "It's not the crows." The night in the arena with Victor flashed in her mind. His stating to everyone that he was going to trap the crows was meant for her. He was baiting her. "I think it's me."

Abby looked at her. "I think so, too. Everyone knows the virus isn't connected to just crows anymore anyway."

Ellie nodded and changed the subject, always mindful of not saying too much about the crows, always being protective. "My grandmother's dying."

"Really? Oh how sad. I forget, how old is she?"

Ellie had to think. "This time around, eighty-five."

"I'm sorry." Abby turned and paused. Bubba was so kind and gentle; just looking at him, who would ever think he'd have this thing about throwing her all the time. "Why oh why is life so difficult?" She pondered the thought of death for a moment, and that led to another, and then another. "I think it's like AIDS and blaming all the gays."

"What is?" Ellie glanced at her.

"The crows. It's not their fault they have it, or that mosquitoes zoom in on them and spread it everywhere. The blue jays either. And I don't think it's because of their lifestyle."

Ellie shrugged. "They're meat eaters. People don't like that in a bird."

"So." Abby led Bubba into the other crossties. "Eagles eat meat. Imagine the uproar if they were the only ones responsible for carrying it. Our national bird."

Ellie pretended to shudder. "Oh wow, we won't even go there. One does cleanup, the other one kills."

Victor walked past them just then, his head cocked like radar to try to hear what they were saying. Ellie gave him something to think about. "I wouldn't tell anyone what you heard. At least no one here."

* * *

The arena was empty. No visible reason for Damian and Bubba to spook. Yet as soon as they entered, both horses took on a stance horsemen know only too well; that prey-predator kind of stance that can lead to trouble. It was the last thing Abby needed at the moment. Any courage she'd managed to muster, vanished in a flash.

"I can't do this," she insisted. "Look at him." Bubba resembled a Sherman tank revved in low gear ready to charge up a hill. "He's going to dump me for sure."

"No, he's not. Now come on, get on." Ellie mounted Damian and had to take a good hold to keep him from trotting off. A door slammed shut in the distance.

Abby put her foot in her stirrup, changed her mind, and took it back out. She drew a deep breath. Glancing around the arena made her dizzy.

"Don't think about it. Just do it," Ellie said, as Damian danced in place.

Abby nodded, easier said than done. She climbed up and lowered herself gingerly into the saddle. Bubba stood staring, nostrils flared and wide-eyed. Ellie rode Damian up next to them. "Come on, walk along."

"I can't," Abby said. "I'm going to throw up."

"Good, then throw up and get it over with," Ellie said, adding. "Only do it that way." She motioned to the other side and Abby laughed nervously.

For the first few minutes, all was well. The horses worked obediently, though on-the-muscle, until suddenly, for no apparent reason, Bubba jumped sideways and crashed into Damian. Ellie's and Abby's legs and stirrups banged into one another's with a clang. And both horses started acting up

"Oh, shit. Oh, shit," Abby kept saying as Ellie repeated, "Be calm, be calm." Ellie grabbed hold of Bubba's inside rein, and pulled him even closer, his head now over Damian's neck and practically in her lap. "Get after him, come on. Get his attention."

"I can't! What if he bucks me off?"

"He won't! Come on, I won't let him. Get after him!"

Abby thumped Bubba with her outside leg, which had him bouncing off Damian again, who seemed to rather be enjoying himself, dancing and snorting, and tossing his head.

"Keep getting after him. Get after him!"

Abby got brave, thumped Bubba again, and tightened the reins. Together, with Ellie still leading Bubba, and Damian in a full extended trot under Ellie's one-handed stranglehold, they made their way down the side of the arena and around the turn. Bubba tried bolting again, a maneuver that sent him careening into Damian's shoulder. Damian pinned his ears in retaliation and tried to bite him. During all this something caught Ellie's attention. Something shiny. Something high. Something in the hayloft.

One second it was there. And the next, gone.

"Did you see that?"

"What?"

Ellie loosened her hold of Bubba's rein coming out of the turn so she could straighten his head and urged Abby to keep him moving. When both horses were striding strong, practically in tandem, Ellie ventured another glance over her shoulder into the rafters. Nothing.

Another trip around, still nothing. "I'm going to let you go now, just keep him trotting. Okay?"

Abby nodded with a tremendous look of determination on her face. From this point on, it was just a regular ride. Bubba behaved himself beautifully. Damian, on the bit, was his usual handful. Working from opposite ends of the arena, both horses, upon Ellie's lead and Abby's following, went through the paces of walk, trot, and canter on command. Abby even trotted Bubba over the cavalletti, still set up from someone's schooling session earlier in the day.

"That was awesome!" she said, smiling proudly. "And I *didn't* get dumped!"

When they'd both cooled their horses and rubbed them down and put them away, Ellie headed out into the arena for another look in the rafters. Abby was right on her heels. "What do you think you saw anyway?"

"I don't know." She glanced at her watch. If her dad was on time, and wasn't he always, he'd be arriving at the nursing home right about now. She had to leave.

* * *

Grandma Betty looked up and smiled as Ellie entered the room. Ellie's father had his back to them and was staring out the window. When he heard footsteps, he turned and acknowledged Ellie with his trademark greeting; an exhaustive sigh. Always, that sigh. Ellie searched Grandma

Betty's eyes for a sense of how the visit was going, how the good-byes were going, the farewells.

"I was just telling your grandmother that'll she probably outlive me," her father said, coming over and giving Ellie a kiss on the cheek. "She looks marvelous. Doesn't she look marvelous?"

Ellie nodded. She did look marvelous. Leave it to Grandma Betty to look this good to die.

"The aide is heating up a little something Jewel sent for dinner." No sooner said, than a bowl of chili-con-carne arrived. Jewel's specialty.

"She's sorry she couldn't be here today."

Grandma Betty nodded and took a whiff.

"She wonders if Saturday would be a good day to visit."

Grandma Betty shrugged her frail shoulders. Two days from now, perfect. An empty room is all they'd find. "Tell her not to feel bad if I'm not here. It's nothing personal."

Ellie's father shook his head. "Now, Ma…" he said, her one and only son, her only living child. "Didn't we just talk about this?"

Grandma Betty nodded dutifully. Then much to Ellie's surprise, she blew on a spoonful of chili, held it for the longest time in front of her, wobbling, without spilling a drop, and brought it slowly to her mouth.

The aide left the room. Ellie turned as her dad followed the woman out. "Here," she heard him say. "Just a little something as a way of saying thank you."

The woman stared at the $5 bill. "No, really. That's not necessary. Besides, we're not allowed to…."

Ellie edged closer to her grandmother's side. "Grandma, you don't have to eat that if you don't want."

"I know. It's rather good though," Grandma Betty said, doling out another spoonful and this time spilling quite a bit along the way. "I like the cinnamon she puts in it."

Ellie sat down next to her bed.

"Would you like some, dear?"

Ellie shook her head.

"He'll be leaving shortly anyway."

True. Within a minute, to be precise. "Can't you stay a little longer?" Ellie asked, for her grandmother's sake, for her sake.

"Actually, I would if I could. You know that," her dad said, glancing at his watch. "I'll try and stop back. Right now I've got to get across town and be there within the hour." Ellie waited outside the room and then walked with him as far as the nurses' station.

He seemed genuinely moved by whatever Grandma Betty may have said to him in private, but not to the extent that it changed his plans. "She'll be fine," he assured Ellie. "She's a tough old broad. She always has been. It'll take a lot more than this to do her in."

"A lot more of what?" Ellie wanted to ask. But it wasn't often she saw her Dad emotional. It rendered her speechless. She watched him walk down the hallway and make the turn. He didn't look back and wave. He didn't look back at all.

Grandma Betty had finished the bowl of chili-con-carne by the time Ellie returned to the room. Another surprise. "It was really very tasty."

Ellie smiled. She looked so happy, and yet at the same time…. "Do you still want to go?"

"Oh yes," Grandma Betty said, wiping her mouth with a tissue. "I'm ready."

~ 12 ~

It was no easy task, getting Grandma Betty out the door. First, she had to be put back into bed to have her clothes changed, her diaper changed, and her medications administered. She had to be bundled up so as not to get a chill. She had to have her nitroglycerine patch updated. She had to have her shoes removed and her slippers put back on, since her feet were swollen and starting to hurt. She had to have a moment to catch her breath, and then another minute or two to "get her bearings." All the while she kept saying please and thank you to the aide and nurse, like a good little girl. "Thank you, thank you, thank you." Until finally, she was deemed ready, and then not one spare wheelchair could be found. Two aides searched everywhere. Grandma Betty didn't have one of her own and Physical Therapy was locked up tight for the evening, so they ended up borrowing one from another resident. The man let them use it begrudgingly.

"Don't adjust the legs!" he barked. "They're just the way I like them. That's my wheelchair."

Grandma Betty heard the fuss. "I'll bet I could walk with my walker," she insisted.

"I'm sure you could," Ellie said. "But I'd feel better this way." Not to mention the floor nurse's insistence that this would be the only way. The woman removed the footrests.

"I really wish you'd change your mind. When will you have her back?"

"Uh...." Ellie looked to Grandma Betty.

"An hour, hour and a half. Why? It's not like I'll be missed."

"Oh, Betty, you'll be missed. Trust me."

Ellie brought her car around to the back door and rang the buzzer. She peered in the window. Grandma Betty had been parked in the hall by the nurses' station, and looked so tiny, so weak; her feet dangled halfway up the legs of the wheelchair. Her head was tilted to the side, her hands in her lap.

Ellie rang the buzzer again, overcome with a sudden urgency. "Now. Let me get her out of here now."

An aide appeared from one of the rooms and wheeled Grandma Betty toward her.

"Ellie? Ellie, is that you?"

"No, your granddaughter's right outside. Here she is."

The transfer from the wheelchair to the car was not without its own share of drama. Grandma Betty was in such a hurry to stand on her own two feet, she gathered up all her energy too soon. The nurse's aide hadn't locked the wheelchair firmly yet. It started to move backwards, taking Grandma Betty with it, half in and half out. And even though it moved at a snail's pace, it caught the aide and

Ellie by surprise. Each little paddle-shuffle of Grandma Betty's feet sent her sliding further and further away and closer and closer to the ground.

It struck Grandma Betty as funny and she started laughing, which added momentum and only made things worse as the aide scrambled to avoid stepping on her feet and right the situation, and her. "Be serious, Betty. Now cut that out."

Grandma Betty laughed even more. "I am serious! As serious as a heart attack," she said, and loved saying that. It was one of her second husband Dutch's favorite sayings. Dutch. How long had it been since she'd thought of him. Oh, what a man. Oh, what a lover. When she stopped laughing, there was still a smile on her face from thinking about him

"Now don't do that again," the aide said. "Understand?"

Grandma Betty nodded. It was because he was such a good lover that that slut Wanda was always after him. Even after he and Betty had been married for years. "The bitch!" Always cooking up things for him at the Legion when Betty wasn't around, and....

"Who me? You calling me a bitch? I'm only trying to get you in the car. Here, put your hands around my neck."

"It's Wanda," Grandma Betty said, clasping her fingers behind the aide's neck and holding on for dear life. "She was the bitch." Course, Dutch would have had to at one point show her just how good a good lover he really was, and.... "Good lovers back then didn't mean doing all that fancy stuff they do now either. That man could do it with his eyes. He had bedroom eyes," she said. And now it was the aide who laughed.

"Betty, you crack me up sometimes."

"Me, too," Grandma Betty said, while being plopped into the passenger seat of Ellie's car. As little as she was, she was all dead weight. "Where's my granddaughter? Ellie? Ellie, did you leave?"

"No, Grandma, I'm right here." Ellie felt a wave of apprehension wash over her. What had she gotten herself into? She glanced over her shoulder into the nursing home. It wasn't too late to change her mind.

Yes, it was.

Grandma Betty folded her arms across her chest and stared straight ahead. Woman on a mission.

"Now Betty, you behave," were the aide's parting words. "You hear."

Grandma Betty saluted her. "Ariva derche."

Ellie got in behind the wheel.

* * *

First on the agenda was Grandma Betty's request for a drive-by at the American Legion Hall. "A drive-by." That's just how she'd put it, voice low, and her peering out the window with her tiny little head barely clearing the dash. "Go slow, please. I want to see if I recognize any of the cars."

Ellie smiled sadly. It had to be at least fifteen years since her grandmother had been to the Legion. Did she really think...? Ellie slowed traffic to a virtual halt. When the car behind them honked, she motioned for its driver to go around. The man flipped her off in passing.

His actions barely got a glance. "You okay, Grandma?"

She looked paler all of a sudden, weaker.

"I don't recognize a single one."

"Maybe it's too early."

"Nah, maybe it's too late. Maybe they're all dead."

Two more cars passed

"I'll tell you though. We had some grand parties after some of them funerals. There's nothing like a military funeral, Ellie."

"I thought you didn't like funerals, Grandma."

"Oh, I never said that. When they play them Taps...." She pressed her hand to her heart. "It gets me every time."

Ellie smiled. Grandma Betty was still straining to see over the dashboard. "Do you want to go look again?"

"You don't mind?"

"No." Ellie drove around the block. She approached the Legion even more slowly this second time. "You sure you don't want me to drive in?"

"Yes. It's a hard parking lot to maneuver."

Ellie chuckled. Grandma Betty had a reputation for being hell on wheels. Stone boulders, detour signs, garage doors, buildings, they'd all been fair game. "Maybe if I'm careful."

"Okay, but it's pretty tricky in the back. You'll have to watch."

The rear parking lot was little more than an alley, definitely a challenge. Ellie could only imagine the mishaps if someone had experienced a few too many spirits.

"Oh, look!" Grandma Betty said. "There's Kalamazoo's station wagon."

"Kalamazoo?"

"He was from Michigan. Big guy! Sloppy as can be, but nice as hell."

Ellie nodded. The description fit the car's MO. "It's a little dirty."

"The man was a pig."

Ellie laughed. The car looked abandoned.

"He'd have to at least be in his late 80's, early 90's. I can't believe he's still driving."

He's probably not, Ellie thought.

"Good old Kalamazoo. That man could sing like Dean Martin." Her voice cracked, as memories swirled in her mind. "I'll tell you, Ellie. He sounded just like him."

"Do you want me to go see if he's inside?"

"No." Grandma Betty wiped her eyes. "Do you have anything to write on? Maybe I'll leave him a note."

Ellie found an old envelope; it would have to do, and leaned close. She loved her grandmother's handwriting. It was so elegant, even with the slight tremor in her hand. "Good handwriting is the sign of a true lady," she'd read once.

Dear Kalamazoo, Betty Boop here. I saw your car and just wanted to say hello!

"Betty Boop?"

Grandma Betty shrugged. "If I put my real name, he might not remember me. Betty Boop he'll remember."

Ellie secured the note under one of the station wagon's windshield wipers, and got back in her car to the rumble of distant thunder. She glanced at the gas gauge. Half empty, half full. "Where to now?" Grandma Betty had mentioned the cemetery earlier, but Ellie wasn't sure if she'd been serious or not.

Apparently she was. Grandma Betty yawned. "Might as well get it over with."

Grandma Betty dozed on the way and looked smaller and smaller, frailer and frailer, at each intersection. The cemetery was near the lake, a little over a half-hour drive, and easy enough to find. It was in the direct path of the storm.

"Closed at Dusk," the sign read, but thankfully there was no gate to keep them out. The honor system. "Grandma." Ellie touched her arm gently. "We're here."

Grandma Betty opened her eyes and looked around. "Well, I'll be damned. Look where I ended up."

Ellie laughed.

"And on such a lovely evening." A big bolt of lightning tore through the sky. "Take this road to your right." It wound around a mausoleum, behind a maintenance shed, down a little hill, and dead-ended into a barricaded drop-off to the lake. "Right here."

Ellie parked close, took her hands off the wheel, and there they sat, as if they were going to spread wings and fly.

Both were silent for a moment. Ellie wondered what Grandma Betty was thinking, and Grandma Betty not thinking much at all. It was the most peaceful feeling she'd had in years; away from the nursing home, away from the sick and dying, the endless days.

The storm was about to hit, the waves offshore picking up momentum. "I love the rain," Grandma Betty said. And just like that, as if giving thanks for her devotion, here it came!

Something in the rearview mirror caught Ellie's eyes. A flock of crows scattering. She smiled.

*　　*　　*

Ellie's father returned to the nursing home to find them gone, and had a fit. He didn't have time for this nonsense. His mother and daughter knew he was coming back and they shouldn't have left. He had fifty million other things he could be doing, needed to be doing, besides sitting here at this "goddamn nursing home." He'd cut a client short on the phone. He'd missed a fax that he'd have to drive all the way back to the office to get. He needed to have it with him for his flight first thing in the morning. He'd left a pile of proposals stacked on his desk....

A nurse brought him a cup of coffee, the third since his return. "I'm sure they'll be back soon. Your mother was not doing well. She'll tire easily."

He nodded and sighed.

"Perhaps you'd like to watch a little television."

"Do you have cable?"

"As a matter of fact, we do." The nurse turned the set on, handed him the remote, and left the room.

The reception was bad. The cable connector wasn't screwed in all the way. He fixed that, then adjusted the color. It had too much green. Then he flipped through the channels, found the one he wanted, and sat down in his mother's chair. It smelled like her. All powdery, flowery. What was that perfume she used to wear? He watched the message scrawl across the bottom of the screen. One of those annoying weather alerts. The weather people never got the forecast right anyway, so why bother paying attention?

He leaned his head back. It had been a long day. A good day, but a long day. He'd accomplished a lot. Again, he thought of the downside, everything he'd left undone or missed to rush back over here. And now, to make matters worse, he just realized he hadn't eaten lunch, let alone his being late for dinner. He got up and looked in his mom's fridge. Pudding, Jello, cheese strips. He checked her top drawer, the most likely place for a spoon. There were several. A chocolate pudding, a cherry banana Jello, and two cheese strips later, he sat back down and changed channels. John Wayne, one of his earlier ones. He looked like he couldn't have been more than twenty-five.

Two nurse's aides started into the room and backed out.

It felt odd, his sitting there without his mom. Without his daughter. Ellie was almost always there when he'd visit. Where the hell were they? He glanced at his mom's slippers under her bed. Red, fluffy and red. If he remembered correctly, Jewel had bought them for her.

Jewel, she'd be waiting. He glanced at his watch, eight-fifteen.

He finished his coffee and just sat there. The one thing he never had to do was worry about Ellie. Not in the usual sense that is. She had her strange ways, but overall never gave him trouble and, "Always managed to land on her feet." Jewel had done the best she could to fill Ellie's mother's place. She'd stepped right in after they married, took her under her wing, and did a good job raising her. It's not every woman that would accept another woman's child as her own. But Jewel was special that way. He hated it whenever he disappointed her, like now, with her waiting dinner. If his mother and daughter weren't back by eight-thirty, he was just going to have to leave.

A sound in the hall distracted him, and he looked up to see an elderly woman enter the room, quivering, her arms outstretched like a Frankenstein. Drool slithered from her open mouth. "You're doing good, April," an aide at her side said. "Just a little bit further."

It was too much. He stopped at the nurse's station, left a message, and vanished.

* * *

Though it was close to Grandma Betty's usual bedtime, not to mention her declining state, she was enjoying a second wind. They weren't a grandmother who was dying at a cemetery and a granddaughter holding on to her every last moment. They were children at the park, playing games with the wipers as they weathered the storm. Off... On... Delay... Low... And fast as they could go! It was euphoric!

"Oh, look!" Ellie pointed to a perfectly straight bolt of vertical lightning out over the lake directly in front of them.

Both jumped with the almost instantaneous boom! They'd known it was coming, and yet it startled them both.

Grandma Betty laughed and then sighed. "I'm going to miss you, Ellie."

Ellie nodded, wanted to say, "Me, too," but couldn't trust her voice right then, couldn't trust herself. She couldn't imagine life without her Grandma. Her heart ached at the thought of it.

"So what's new with the Dildo?"

Ellie laughed. Leave it to Grandma Betty. "Oh...." She hesitated. "He's fine I guess."

Grandma Betty shook her head at the look on Ellie's face. "You got it bad, girl. That's so sad."

Ellie shrugged. It seemed like ages since she'd seen him, and yet it was only just yesterday. "He's really nice, Grandma. Most of the time at least. I don't know why you don't like him."

Grandma Betty glanced away and winced.

"You okay?"

She nodded, but held her side. "I wish I knew what to expect."

"Me, too."

~ 13 ~

Abby sat down with a book Ellie had loaned her; the one with the chapter about "becoming a crow." With the storm outside and her husband out of town for a few days, it was the perfect night to curl up with a good book. She contemplated the preface. The author seemed like a neat lady. "For as long as I can remember," the woman wrote, "I have felt close to nature. I have felt the aliveness of each unique entity, whether holding a stone in my hand and feeling its warmth or coolness, drinking in a magnificent skyfull of sunset, or quietly watching deer moving alertly through the forest with indescribable grace and elegance.

"Some years ago, these imageries started nudging me. Eight of them emerged, and then I set them aside, involved with other things in my life. Early last winter, they began nudging me again, only harder, seeming determined to be born into the world. Since then, they've been ever-present, calling me back if I'm too long away. This book you hold in your hand is the culmination of that birthing process."

Abby gazed again at the cover, a welcoming summer path in a lush forest. The book had been a gift to Ellie, the inscription reading, "For your birthday. I was there! Love, Grandma Betty." Chapter Eight was about the crow. Abby sipped her coffee and started reading.

"Become a crow.... Experience your body.... Black, with shimmerings of deep blue & purple.... Look around from your roosting place high in a pine tree.... You can see for a long distance.... On one side, the woods offer roosting trees and shelter for assembling.... On the other, farm lands open wide, with special opportunities for food.... And beyond, the noisy highways of constant movement, where animals often die....

It's dawning. You stretch your wings, and become aware of your hunger.... You take off from your roost, with a relaxed CAW CAW CAW, inviting others to join you in your morning search for food. Experience your wings as they move slowly and deliberately in flight, with regular even wingbeats against supporting air.... Feel the air parting as you move through.... Others of your friends are flying too, in a loosely-formed flock. You fly toward the cornfields. This is the time of seedsprouting.... No two-leggeds in sight. Only the still sticks dressed like a two-legged. You scornfully land on its hat, waiting for the others to gather... Now you all settle on the field, savoring the tender sprouts.... A sharp crack reverberates. A two-legged with a killing stick! CAW! CAW! CAW! CAW! Great danger! The dispersal call is given, and the flock scatters instantly. Your wings beat hard and evenly, carrying you away from the field....

As you fly, you hear the call of a friend, and you both turn toward the highway... You settle together onto the dirt near the road. No newly-killed animals in sight here, but you feel the vibrations with your feet as the big, many-wheeled, noisy ones pass by. You exchange glances, and wait.... The ground surface near you stirs, and an earthworm emerges, brought to the surface by the vibrations. You and your friend feed, and wait.... Feed, and wait. Grateful for food.... When your hunger is appeased, you spread your wings, again committing yourself to the supportive air. Drawing your legs up under your body, you rise above the incessant and oppressive din, and again enjoy the loveliness of flying.... The subtle control of direction.... The sunlight on your wings.... You are aware of others from your flock, hearing their individual call as they forage for food....

Your friend whizzes by, playfully inviting you to chase. You accept, increasing the force of your wings against the air, climbing, turning, diving, trying to anticipate your friend's moves. Calling out in the challenge and enjoyment.... Finally, energy spent, you both settle onto branches in adjacent trees, cawing to each other.... Resting... In the meadow below, cows are drowsing. You decide to play some more. Launching from your branch, you swoop down over the unsuspecting cows, and tweak at the nearest ear.... Returning to your branch, you caw your mischievous joy. Your friend caws his approval, then leaves his roost, and duplicates your performance. Together, you caw raucously at the hapless cows....

Suddenly, you hear the assembly call! Predator! Predator! Instantly you fly toward the call. A hawk has been detected in the flock's territory, and is being mobbed, amidst clamoring cawing. You join in, as your family and friends, in great and persistent numbers, fly at the hawk, loudly threatening and harassing, making clear their territory and their intention that he leave.... The hawk, relinquishing, and deciding to try again another day, flies away from your roosting woods.... Across the fields.......

You and the flock settle on your roosting places, victorious and self-satisfied.... There is some bickering, here and there, over a favored roost, accompanied by threat calls.... The young crows take this time to play.

You decide to take one last flight in the fast-changing light of the setting sun. Your wingspan is wide and sure.... As you survey the ground beneath you, an object glints in the slanting rays of the sun. You fly lower to investigate.... Your inquisitiveness brings you to rest beside a round, sparkling object connected to a long, bright chain. You pick it up in your beak, and push off into the air. The chain comes loose and drops away, and you carry your glittering prize across to the edge of the meadow, to the base of a small fir tree. You look around to see if you are being observed.... It seems safe. You set your treasure down, pushing and turning it with your beak. It is beautiful! The sun is below the horizon, so you carefully bury your shiny new find beneath the small tree.......

Your wings lift you smoothly in flight, and you enjoy the evening coolness as you soar and descend.... Now you return to the sheltering woods, and amidst your flock, find a comfortable roosting place for the night.... Your friend nearby sends you a soft, acknowledging CAW.... Your heart holds happiness at your place in the Universe.... You are tired.... And content.... You look forward to returning to your new-found discovery.... Your tiredness and contentedness blend, and you settle on your roost into a peaceful, quiet rest......."

Abby sat back and smiled.

~ 14 ~

The storm vanished and in its wake, a beautiful calm descended. Ellie opened the windows. "I love the night," she told Grandma Betty. "I often wonder why I wasn't born at night."

"I was born at the stroke of midnight," Grandma Betty said. "Can you believe that?"

Ellie smiled. Yes, she really could.

"My mother said right as the clock chimed twelve, I emerged, my hair curly as can be. She'd never had curly-haired children before. I was her eleventh and final child."

"How old was she?" Ellie had heard variations of this story before, but never tired of it.

"Thirty-two. My father was forty-three. He was a mean son of a bitch. Always whipping us for something or other."

Grandma Betty was the last of her brothers and sisters alive.

"How did your mother...?"

"How did she keep him away?"

Ellie nodded.

"She slept with a shotgun by her pillow."

"You sure it wasn't a revolver?"

"Nope, it was a shotgun. Full of salt and buckshot. I watched her load it myself."

"Did she ever shoot him?" This was always Ellie's favorite part.

"Yep, once." They both recited the end of the story. "And he didn't sit down for a week."

The two of them laughed. Ellie didn't know if it was a true story or not, at least not all of it, but she always laughed at its familiar ending. She'd only ever seen one portrait of her great grandfather, and he indeed did look mean.

Ellie checked her watch; it was getting close to ten o'clock. "Grandma, I don't think we can stay here too much longer."

"No?"

Ellie shook her head. "Did you have a particular reason for wanting to come to the cemetery?"

Grandma Betty sat for a moment, thinking. "I'm sure I did." Memory loss was one of her few regrets. "I knew I should have made a list. Now why can't I remember? What was it?"

Ellie gave her a moment.

"Oh forget it," Grandma Betty said. "I can't remember. Let's go."

"You sure?"

"Yes."

Ellie started the car and glancing out her side mirror, noticed a set of headlights coming from the far side of the mausoleum. Oh no, probably a cop on patrol, she thought. Or worse. Would the nursing home have reported her grandmother missing by now? Had someone made note of her license plate number? No. Why would they? Was the patrol just routine? Probably. Even so, how would she explain the reason for their presence?

They had to get out of there fast.

"Shouldn't you turn your lights on, dear?"

"No," Ellie said. "I see really well in the dark."

Ellie maneuvered the narrow, winding roads perfectly, much to Grandma Betty's delight. "We could be grave robbers. Gravediggers. Sin eaters." They were invisible, a blanket of night covering them; a shroud of black. They were all the way to the entrance and pulling out when her grandmother remembered. "Wait!"

"I'm sorry, Grandma. We can't." The patrol car had taken a right at the last crossroad, and instead of heading toward the back of the cemetery, was winding its way toward the front, toward them. "We have to leave."

Grandma Betty was silent until they got to the first intersection and Ellie had turned her lights on. "I wonder if I'll still be around in the morning."

"Why?" Ellie hadn't thought that far ahead. "What's the matter?"

"Oh, nothing." Grandma Betty peered over the door out the side window, so small, so child-like.

"Grandma, come on. What?"

"Well, it's just that I think I really have to go back."

"To the nursing home?"

"No, to the cemetery."

Ellie suppressed a sigh and paused. When Grandma Betty didn't say anything more, she reached over and gently squeezed her hand. "Okay."

She turned the car around, approached the cemetery cautiously, and kept right on going. The cop car was still there and, if she weren't mistaken, on the lookout.

"Shit!"

Grandma Betty strained to see. "Maybe if we wait a while."

Ellie glanced at her and couldn't help smiling. She was on an adventure. She was having fun.

They pulled into a parking lot about a block away, and watched and waited. The cop car never budged. "He's probably one of those slackers Diablo talks about. I'll bet he's just going to sit there till the shift change."

Another cop car pulled in and parked.

They're on to us, Ellie thought, and was just about to make a break, when suddenly both cop cars pulled out and went the other way.

"Oh what luck," Grandma Betty said.

Ellie wasn't so sure. She'd been around Diablo too long. "If they think we're teenagers...."

"Then they're mistaken," Grandma Betty said, and laughed. She was indeed having fun!

"Maybe I should get a hold of Diablo."

"Why?"

"I don't know. But I don't think we should go back there on our own." Nor did she want to get arrested for trespassing. She was pretty sure they were still in his precinct. Wouldn't this be fun to explain.

Ellie looked around for a phone booth, and spotted one on the other side of the lot about twenty yards away. She pulled up fairly close to it and though she probably could have reached it from inside the car, she got out to make the call. She leaned back in. "Are you warm enough, Grandma? Do you want me to turn the heat on?"

"No, I'm fine."

Ellie dialed and after leaving a message and phone number, sat inside with the door open to wait.

"Will he call you back?"

"I hope so."

"How long?"

"I don't know." No sooner said than the phone rang.

Ellie loved the sound of his voice, even when the tone was contrary.

"Wait a minute. Let me get this straight," he said. "Your grandmother's dying tonight and you two need an escort back into the cemetery."

"Yes."

"I see...." When he paused and cleared his throat, she could almost see him nodding to himself.

"I know it sounds crazy, but she really wants to go back. There's something she needs to do."

"What?"

"I don't know."

Silence.

"So will you come?"

Diablo sighed. "Yeah, I'll be there."

Grandma Betty looked at her as she got back in behind the wheel. "Did I hear you right? Does he think I'm crazy?"

"No, he thinks we're both crazy."

* * *

While they waited, Ellie used the ladies room at an Arby's restaurant and then hurried back to the car. "You sure you don't want anything, Grandma?"

Grandma Betty shook her head. She'd dozed for a few minutes while Ellie was gone and was feeling a little groggy. Disoriented. The pain in her side was back. She drew a breath and tried to right herself with the world. It wasn't happening. All those clouds....

"Ellie...."

"Yes, Grandma." Ellie leaned close, emotion pouring over her like a flood. Oh God, she thought, this is it. She's dying. "Grandma, are you in pain?"

"A little."

"Oh, God," Ellie gasped, pressing her hand hard to her mouth. "Don't go, Grandma," she wanted to say. "Don't leave me." She touched her grandmother's face, touched her hair. "Oh, please...please..." she begged. "Please...."

As Grandma Betty closed her eyes and leaned her head back, a swirl of images began to go round and round in her mind. Dutch, on his knees, ring in hand. The earthquake. The snowstorm and the chains, the tree down. The baby crying. *It's a boy. Did you want a boy? Yes, I want a boy.*

77

Harold, dear sweet Harold. A father. A funeral. A hearse. David. *I take this man, David. I do. Dearly beloved....*

Ellie scrambled to reach over the seat for something to cover her; she was shivering. Why hadn't she brought the patchwork-quilt? A horse blanket. It was all she had; it would have to do. She covered Grandma Betty as gently as she could, tears flowing, hands shaking. "Don't call her back," she kept saying to herself. "Don't call her back. Don't call her back." Oh, Grandma, I love you....

Grandma Betty gripped Ellie's hand and held it tight, tighter, and tighter....

And then the images stopped.

The pain that ravaged her, ceased. It was gone.

She could breathe again.

"Grandma? Grandma, are you okay?"

She nodded. "Yes, I think so. What is that awful smell?"

Ellie laughed nervously and wiped her eyes. "It's Damian's blanket. It needs to be washed."

"I should say so."

They both laughed. A reprieve, they'd been given a reprieve. Grandma Betty pointed out the window and Ellie turned to look. A police car had just turned into the cemetery.

Diablo.

Ellie tossed the blanket into the back seat and pulled her car in behind his. He sat for a moment, talking on the scanner, then got out and with a veteran touch of his hand to the gun on his hip, walked toward them.

Grandma Betty shook her head in awe. "None too hard on the eyes, now is he?" They watched his every move, the way he walked, the way he glanced around...the way he didn't glance around. He was all business when he approached Ellie's door.

She put her window down.

"Diablo, this is my Grandma Betty. Grandma Betty, Diablo."

Diablo nodded, but in such a way, Grandma Betty would have sworn it was a bow. A very gentlemanly bow, rather Zorro-like.

Ellie feared from the smile on her grandmother's face that she was about to call him "the Dildo" and diverted her attention. "Where is it that you want to go in the cemetery, Grandma?"

She had to think for a second. "Uh, to the back, where we were before."

"It's by the drop-off," Ellie said, "behind the mausoleum. Do you want to follow me?"

Diablo gave her a look, one that said he didn't want any part of this at all, let alone....

"Good, follow me," Ellie said, and quickly rolled up the window in case he was going to object. She waited for him to get into his car then pulled around him and led the way. She could have driven it in her sleep. Past the Michaels, the Smiths, the Epsons, the Websters.... Turn left, where the Coopers lay, the Bagleys....

The view of the lake with a full moon was spectacular. For a moment, after she parked, Ellie almost forgot Diablo was behind her. The moonlight drew her in, calling, calling, shimmering on the water. And suddenly she knew. "This really is good-bye, isn't it Grandma?"

"Yes."

Diablo sat in his police car, waiting and waiting for whatever it was he was waiting and watching over them for, but was totally unprepared for what began to take place. Ellie got out, walked around the car, and opened her grandmother's door. She helped the old woman turn so she faced the outside. She touched her grandmother's face and then her own. She touched her grandmother's heart and then her own. Then she turned and holding something, bent down and gathered a clump of dirt and worked it back and forth in her hands.

He got out of the squad car at that point and walked slowly toward them. Ellie had her back to him and was standing at the drop-off. For a split second, he feared she was going to jump. For a split second, he feared he wouldn't be able to stop her. He could see himself trying to save her. He could see himself jumping off the cliff after her. He could see himself....

It was her voice that made him stop.

"Ashes to ashes," she repeated, at her grandmother's urging.

"To the circle of energy, I return.

"My soul to the universe, of want no more.

"Grant me forever, part of the whole.

"I come as one, no longer alone."

Thus said, she threw the soil from her hands, high over the water, and in an instant it was gone...but for the sound of fluttering wings.

~ 15 ~

Ellie had another favor to ask of Diablo. "Could you find out if there's an APB on my Grandma?"

"An APB?" Under any other circumstances, he might have laughed. Even now, considering what he'd just witnessed, there was a hint of a smile on his face. "Why would you uh...?"

"Because, if we were only going for a ride, which is what we told them, we would have been back a long time ago."

"Why don't you just go back now? That way...."

"We can't. She doesn't want to. She doesn't want to die there."

Grandma Betty had her eyes closed and appeared to be dozing.

"Please."

Diablo hesitated, then shook his head and walked to the squad car. Ellie was right behind him. "Maybe I should phone my dad." Diablo handed her his cell phone and reached for the scanner.

Ellie got her father and Jewel's answering machine. "Dad, this is Ellie. If the nursing home calls, everything's okay. Grandma's with me, and...." She paused, unsure of what to say, how much to say. "Uh, I just wanted you to know everything's okay, all right? I'll call you later."

It was getting close to midnight.

No APB.

Diablo sat in his car looking up at her. "What are you going to do now?"

"I don't know." Ellie glanced at her Grandma, still dozing. "I honestly don't know."

"Well, you'd better come up with something."

"Ellie?"

"I'm right here, Grandma."

Diablo reached for her hand.

"I gotta go," she said. "I don't want her to get frightened."

"What about you, Ellie. Aren't you frightened?"

"No." Oddly enough, she wasn't. Not anymore. "Come on. Come talk to her. I want her to get to know you."

Diablo rolled his eyes and followed.

Grandma Betty was feeling disoriented again, a little worse this time. She also couldn't get comfortable and kept insisting she was in her chair at the nursing home.

"This seat goes back more. Can you put it back more?"

Fortunately the car seat did tilt back, which offered a little more comfort, but then her legs started cramping. Out came the horse blanket again. It would have to do. Ellie rolled it into a ball, cleanest side up, and propped Grandma Betty's legs on it.

"How's that?"

"Much better. Thank you."

Diablo scanned the horizon, feeling uncomfortable as well. There they were in a cemetery, which was weird enough considering the hour. Now they were waiting for Ellie's grandmother to die. He imagined trying to explain the sequence of events to his sergeant during one of their weekly briefings at the station. Particularly when he got around to the part about "His girlfriend releasing a bird and...."

"Diablo." Ellie touched his arm. "Do you have a blanket?"

He nodded, refrained from saying, "Your every wish is my command," which is what he was thinking, and went and got it and returned.

Grandma Betty looked up at him. "How's come you've never been to see me before?"

Diablo hesitated. "I work odd hours," was all he could think to say.

"What? Seven days a week?"

"Sometimes," he said, which wasn't necessarily a lie.

"There. How's that?" Ellie tucked the blanket snug around her grandmother and gave her a kiss on the cheek. "Be nice, Grandma," she whispered, and then to Diablo, the same. "Be nice."

Diablo glanced away. Quiet came easy to him. It was a standard joke at the precinct: whenever you wanted a suspect to talk, let Diablo in the room with him. His silence and that stance of his had detainees talking a mile a minute in no time; something about the way he'd cross his arms and set his eyes on the person.

Grandma Betty had a little bit more experience on him though, more years. She was the one doing the staring now and eventually he was the one to speak. "Ellie never invited me."

Ellie couldn't believe he said that. It was the truth, technically, but still. She'd hinted at his coming with her on occasion, but he never offered, never picked up on it, so that was as far as it went. Ellie looked out over the water. Off in the distance, there was a flicker of bright light.

"I hear you bought a Harley."

Diablo nodded. Under the circumstances, even this attempt at conversation, was bizarre.

"What color?"

"Cobalt blue."

Grandma Betty clung to the blanket. "My second husband had a Harley. He didn't have a title for it though, so he only drove it on back streets. I personally think he stole it."

"Grandma…." Ellie laughed.

"It's true, but don't tell your dad."

Ellie laughed again. Even Diablo chuckled.

Grandma Betty looked at the two of them, just looked at them for a moment, then shook her head. Ellie feared what she was about to say, but she didn't say anything. She just shook her head and with a sigh, closed her eyes and dozed off again.

Ellie motioned to a park bench close by, and she and Diablo walked over and sat down. Diablo reached into his shirt pocket for his cigarettes, remembered he'd kicked the habit about three months earlier, and crossed his arms. He drew a deep breath. It had been a long night, a tough shift. Two robberies, a domestic call, and a fatal car accident. A father and his son. The poor little kid was still holding on to his soccer ball.

Ellie linked her arm around his and leaned her head on his shoulder. "Thanks for coming. I appreciate you being here with me."

Diablo nodded slightly. He didn't want to be here. That was obvious. But it was obvious he wasn't leaving either. "So where did the bird come from?"

"What bird?" Ellie yawned.

Diablo stared at her. "You know what bird I'm talking about, Ellie."

She hesitated. "It was just an illusion, Diablo. Everything is an illusion."

"Everything? What do you mean? Life, you, me? The crows?"

Ellie looked at him. That was the first time he'd ever mentioned the crows. She had no idea he even knew of their existence or their connection to her. He'd never acted as if he even knew they were around.

"What was the point? I heard what you said, but what does it mean?"

Ellie paused. There was a sudden chill in the air. "I wonder if I should go run the car heater for a while?"

"In a minute. Answer me first."

"Ellie?"

"I'm right here, Grandma." She turned to Diablo. He still wanted an answer. "I'll explain it all some day, I promise.

But it basically means she's giving up her spirit. Releasing it, so to speak. She doesn't ever want to come back."

"You mean like reincarnation?"

"Yes."

"And that's it? That's all you have to do, say you don't want to come back, and it's done."

Ellie smiled. "Only if you've lived a very long time."

* * *

A short while later, Grandma Betty suffered another wave of pain. This one wasn't nearly as bad, she declared. But if no one minded, she thought she'd like to go to sleep for a bit. "I don't know why, but I'm feeling really tired all of a sudden."

The night couldn't have been quieter. "I hope she doesn't think she has to feel brave with you here," Ellie whispered, when they'd walked a little distance away.

"What's that supposed to mean?" Diablo asked. It's not as if he could leave.

"Nothing. I was just...." She paused, glancing back and feeling helpless. "She hates pain. It's the one thing that frightens her."

Diablo sat back down on the bench and when Ellie just stood there, her saddened gaze fixed on her grandmother, he urged her to sit next to him.

"I don't know what to do," she said.

Neither did he. "You okay?" he asked.

She shrugged. "I want to wrap her in my arms, Diablo. I don't want her to go. She's such an awesome person. Why did I take so long to get to know her?" She bit at her trembling bottom lip.

"Maybe if you take her back to the nursing home and...."

Ellie shook her head. "No, this is what she wants."

The next time Grandma Betty woke, Ellie was all curled up in the driver's seat, asleep at her side. It was near dawn. "You look like an angel," Grandma Betty told her, smiling. And right after that, before Ellie could even sit up and wipe the sleep from her eyes. "So what happened to the Dildo? Did he leave?"

Ellie laughed. He was stretched out on the back seat, and had been asleep as well. Though as light a sleeper as she knew him to be and the way he just stirred, he was surely awake now.

Grandma Betty never looked better, felt better. She was positively radiant. She wasn't in pain. She was well rested. She was ready for more adventure! "Where can we go now? I still have time."

When Ellie suggested the barn, Diablo got up and took a walk into the woods. Ellie waited for him at his car. He returned a little crankier than his usual morning self. "I just pissed in a cemetery. Bet that'll get me into heaven."

Ellie smiled. Grandma Betty's mood had the same euphoric effect on her. Nothing was going to get her down. She wrapped her arms around Diablo's neck and kissed him good-bye. "I'll call you," she said, and then did the strangest thing. She glanced over his shoulder, saw something barely in the dawn, and extended her hand as if touching someone.

"What are you doing?" he asked, turning.

"Nothing," she said, but then did it again, and he shook his head. Whatever she saw, was invisible to him. He was not a believer. If he were, he would have seen it as well. There were spirits everywhere. Some happy. Some sad.

"I'm outta here."

Ellie motioned toward Grandma Betty. "Go talk to her," she whispered.

Diablo sighed and walked over and bent down on one knee, his awkwardness at saying good-bye to a dying woman, apparent. "I'm leaving now," he said. "Is there anything I can do for you? Uh…something you need?"

Grandma Betty smiled. "Nope." She'd just put on her red lipstick and had combed her hair and was raring to go. Ellie used Diablo's cell phone, left another message for her father, same message as before, and off they went.

~ 16 ~

Ellie glanced at her gas gauge only after she turned into the driveway of the farm. It was a little game she played when she was low or about to run out. Don't look till you get where you're going. That way you only worry on your way back. She had a little over a quarter of a tank.

It was perfect timing, too. With the sun up, the horses had probably already been hayed and grained by now. She parked by the stable entrance. "I'll be right back."

She hoped Damian wasn't a mess. Grandma Betty had seen dozens of pictures of him, but never in person before. She wanted him to look his best. She felt like a little child about to show off her favorite toy. Damian nickered at the sound of her voice. "Oh good, you're clean." She grabbed a brush and mane comb, gave him a quick once-over, really quick, and snapped the lead shank onto his halter and led him from his stall.

Victor appeared from out of nowhere. "Aren't you the early riser? Out all night?"

"Good morning," she said, and walked past him.

Grandma Betty was waiting anxiously. There was a time in her life she owned horses herself. Not her actually, but her father. They were workhorses on the farm, two of them. Big Belgians, and both so kind. Her eyes widened as Ellie led Damian toward the car. "Oh my." He was taller than she'd imagined, bigger all over, and so pretty. So shiny black.

"Well, here he is, Grandma. What do you think?"

"He's beautiful," she said, breathlessly.

Damian stood looking around, the newness of his being outside so early, not yet registering. Off in the distance, a flock of crows landed.

"Bring him here. Will he let me pet him?"

Ellie led him closer to the car and opened the door, which spooked Damian a little, but not bad. He backed up a few steps and, at Ellie's urging, came closer. Grandma Betty reached her frail hand out and much to Ellie's surprise and pleasure, Damian nuzzled it. "Oh, he's so soft." He was a giant, looking down on her in the car, a curious giant, who not only nuzzled Grandma Betty's hand, but stretched his neck so he could touch and sniff her face.

"He likes me," she said. "See. He likes me."

Most definitely. It was as if Damian knew her and Grandma Betty knew him. Her, through months and months and months of hearing about him, seeing his pictures, seeing him in her mind. And him, by some sort of association through Ellie, their closeness, their bond. Or perhaps by the sheer fact that she had his scent, thanks to the blanket that had kept her legs from hurting all night.

"Do you want me to turn him out? Do you want to see him run?"

"Yes." Grandma Betty gave him a final pat on the face, and watched as Ellie led him over to the paddock and turned him loose. And oh, how he ran and bucked and kicked. And snorted. And pranced around.

"He is so beautiful, Ellie. I can see why you love him. He's magnificent."

"That he is," Ellie said.

Damian ran to the end of the fence, stopped at the very last second, turned and ran bucking and kicking again, stopping only to raise his head and snort. When he'd finally run himself down, he circled and circled a spot, then buckled his knees and rolled in the moist grass.

"Are you warm enough, Grandma?"

"Yes, quite."

Damian stood and shook himself off, then found another spot and rolled again. And when he got up, he grazed his way over to the fence, where Ellie stood ready to get him and take him back into the barn.

Grandma Betty smiled the entire time, even when she closed her eyes to rest a moment while Ellie was gone. She had lots of stories she wanted to share, to remember. There was the time her dad yelled at her for riding both Belgians in the field, both…standing one leg on each of their backs and keeping them close.

"Betty, now damn it all, you're going to get yourself hurt one of these days! Get down off them right now!"

"But dad…."

"No, don't you dad me! Get down right now! If you'd fallen, you would have been crushed!"

Dutch, too, loved the horses. She laughed. The betting kind. Daily doubles, perfectas, trifectas. And the lottery. He loved to play the lottery.

A crow cawed from nearby, then another, and another. Grandma Betty listened and thought they sounded like magpies. By the time Ellie returned, there was a whole flock of crows lighting down and pecking around in the pasture. Ellie looked at them, and hesitated before getting back into the car. This was her world; she wanted to share all of it with her grandmother.

"Come," she said. "Lolita, come."

Grandma Betty watched as a single crow took flight and soared overhead.

"Lolita, come."

Lolita swooped down and landed on a fence rail and commenced doing a dance; Grandma Betty was thrilled. "Oh, look at her!"

Ellie laughed.

Lolita sashayed up and down the fence, bobbing her head and turning and cocking it this way and that, and then danced some more. "Would you like to see her up close, Grandma?"

"Yes. Will she come?"

"I think so," Ellie said. "But be very still."

Grandma Betty nodded in anticipation as Ellie raised her arm and beckoned Lolita closer.

"Dudabachie," she said, once, waiting, and then again. "Dudabachie."

"What does that mean, Dudabachie?" Grandma Betty wanted to know.

Ellie smiled. "Nothing. Everything. It means she is safe, that I am watching over her. It means pay attention. I made the word up when I was a little girl."

Grandma Betty laughed. "You are still a little girl. This is too much fun for an old woman."

"Come," Ellie said, holding out her hand. "Dudabachie."

Lolita took flight, cawing and cawing, and with a grand swoop, flew to Ellie and landed on the side of her hand.

"Dudabachie," Grandma Betty whispered breathlessly, in awe. "Dudabachie."

From the hayloft in the barn, Victor watched.

"This is Lolita, Grandma. She is a scarlet."

Grandma Betty laughed. "I can see that. She has a smile on her face."

Lolita ruffled her feathers, regarded them both, and then took off in flight, landing far out in the pasture, and cawing and strutting.

"Dudabachie," Grandma Betty said softly to herself. "Indeed."

It was with a sigh that Ellie got behind the wheel, and for a moment the two of them just sat there. Ellie didn't notice Victor still watching, didn't feel the threat. They just sat there, content with one another's company, and treasuring the moment.

Eventually, another car pulled in, then another. The racetrack people. They were always there early. It was time to leave. "Where to now, Grandma?"

"Oh, I'm thinking probably the home."

Ellie looked at her. "Why? Are you in pain?"

"A little." Grandma Betty shrugged. "Not like before."

"Then why?"

"I don't think I should've ate yesterday. It's all Jewel's fault I'm still around."

Ellie smiled. They'd had such fun though. It saddened her to think of taking her grandmother back to the nursing home, knowing how she hated it there, how she didn't want to be there. Knowing....

"But we have to be practical," Grandma Betty insisted. "You have to go to work. You're going to be late as it is.

For some reason, I've been given another day. And I'm sorry to say..." she added, "I think I need my diaper changed."

* * *

Even though Ellie had phoned her father twice to try to avoid a panic, she fully expected to see a squad of cop cars parked outside the nursing home, lights flashing. She expected to see her father's car right along with them, and maybe even Jewel's. She expected mayhem, accusations, and frantic nurses. She expected questions, red tape, a complicated sign-in process. And at the very least, she expected someone to be there to answer the door. She rang the buzzer again and again, and was just about to drive around front, when finally, one of the aides appeared.

"Oh, Ellie," the woman said, talking fast. "It's been a horrible night! Wait here. I'll go get a wheelchair. Everyone's got some kind of flu."

"What'd she say?"

Ellie relayed the message.

"Flu my ass," Grandma Betty said. "It's the food. It's always the food."

The aide returned in a few minutes with help. The transfer from the car to the wheelchair was quick and efficient. Ellie trailed along after them to Grandma Betty's room. In a matter of seconds, the aides had her in bed and were gathering things to give her a sponge bath.

Ellie edged up next to her side and kissed her good-bye. "Grandma...?"

"I'm fine, Ellie," she whispered. "Don't worry. I'll have no part of dying in the daytime."

Ellie hugged her gently, always mindful of her frail bones. "I'll come by after work," she said, and looked back at her from the door.

Grandma Betty waved. "Go," she said, and then held her nose. Ellie laughed, only to turn and come face to face with the ex-army nurse, who was not in a good mood.

"Perfect. You're still here," she said. "The DN wants to see you."

"The DN?"

"Director of Nursing. Down the hall and take a right."

Ellie stopped off in the ladies room, washed up, and entered the DN's office with great trepidation. All her fears proved warranted. "I was just about to place a call to the police."

Ellie apologized over and over, blamed it all on car trouble; Grandma Betty's suggestion, and sat receiving a lecture. "Beds are held for only so long unoccupied, particularly Medicaid beds. We have a waiting list a mile long. This is highly irregular. She is our responsibility. You should have phoned."

"I phoned my father."

"Yes, and thankfully he had the courtesy to phone us. However, if we'd been given information as to where you were, we could have sent transport out, and…."

Ellie nodded. That was precisely why she hadn't. She'd feared as much.

"What if something had happened to your grandmother? What if you'd needed medical assistance? What if she'd fallen or hurt herself? What if she'd had an attack or died?"

Ellie stared.

"Your grandmother *is* all right, isn't she?"

"Yes."

The rest of Ellie's morning followed suit. She had three messages from her father waiting for her at the office, and barely time to glance through them when there he stood, looming over her desk. This wasn't the first time he'd ever visited her at work. It was the first time he'd ever arrived angry, however. Her boss excused herself and left the room.

"What were you thinking?" he hissed.

"Uh…."

"That's right. You weren't."

"I only…."

"No, Ellie. Don't bother! I don't want to hear it. I just left your grandmother's and she told me the whole story. Do not think you're going to do this again. Do you hear me? Don't ever do this again!"

Ellie nodded, full well knowing that if her grandmother asked, she *would* do it again. There was no doubt in her mind. The only question would be, how?

~ 17 ~

Grandma Betty slept off and on most of the day, and toward evening, started feeling like death again. It was a depressing thought, knowing this was where it was going to take place. But then again, she did promise her son, "Not to make trouble."

"Betty! Betty, what are you doing?"

"I'm not sure." She was sideways in bed and dangling her arms over the edge as if paddling a boat. "I guess I was dreaming."

"Here." The aide got her straightened around and back onto the pillow. "My word, you could have fallen on your head."

"I think I've done that before."

The aide laughed. "Knowing you, probably. I swear, Betty, sometimes...."

Grandma Betty smiled. "Has my granddaughter been here?"

"Yes, and she's coming back. She said when you woke to tell you that she'll be back around ten-thirty."

Grandma Betty nodded and then noticed something. "Oh my, look at my fingernails. Aren't they pretty?" They were the brightest red she'd ever seen.

"Your granddaughter did them. She asked if it was okay when you were sound asleep, and I said sure. She sang to you, Betty. She sang you a song about a horse named *Wildfire*. It was the sweetest sound, all soft and her believing you could hear her. I swear, Betty, it was the sweetest sound I ever heard."

"I love that song. "

"I know. That's what she said when she saw I heard her."

Grandma Betty closed her eyes and could hear Ellie singing it again and again.

"April's down watching the movie."

"Who?"

"April," the aide said. "Your roommate. Do you want your TV on?"

"No, that's okay. I won't be able to hear Ellie sing then."

"Yes, you will. I told you, she'll be back around ten-thirty. You rest now, hear?"

"Am I wet?"

"No, hon. I just checked you. You get some rest now."

* * *

The inevitable happened. Ellie's car ran out of gas. Fortunately, it was on the way home from work. She had her paycheck and the bank first and then the gas station wasn't that far to walk. It did put her late at the laundromat though. And the place was packed.

Friday night yet. "Don't you people have anywhere else to go?" she asked.

Regulars, they all laughed.

"And you," she said, to a sleepy teen. "No leaving here between wash and dry."

She made change for whoever needed it, washed a load of laundry herself, Damian's blanket, and tried keeping busy for the next three hours. She swept the floor. She wiped off all the washers and dryers. She emptied the trash. She even washed the windows. Old Mr. Franklin from upstairs said she was like a "Freight train going through Richmond." Everything in her path got cleaned. When ten o'clock came around, time to lock up and drive to the nursing home, she was exhausted. She rolled all the windows down in her car and turned up the volume on her radio to try and revive herself.

She'd never been to the nursing home this late before and was surprised upon arriving to find it somewhat transformed. It had an entirely different feel to it. Everyone was in his or her rooms, the lights dimmed here and there. No one sat lined up in wheelchairs in the hallways and gathering areas, looking frightened or confused, slumped over or tied in. No one was crying. The place seemed rather peaceful. Even the nurses and aides seemed more subdued, happier.

"Just wait," Grandma Betty told her after a hug and a kiss. "At midnight, the howling begins."

Ellie chuckled. "Oh, Grandma."

"I'm serious. Ask April."

April was sound asleep. Ellie laughed at the suggestion, another obvious joke. She pulled a chair up close to her grandmother's bed. "How are you?" she asked softly.

"Fine. But don't worry, there's no need to whisper. April can't hear. They take her hearing aids out at night."

Ellie fussed with her grandmother's blankets.

"I'm not bleeding anymore."

"Good."

"Apparently I'm peeing again though."

Ellie smiled. This was it, the best they could do. Her grandmother was resigned to the fact she'd be dying here, and Ellie promised to be with her.

"What are the nurses telling you?"

Ellie hesitated. "That it won't be long."

"Hours, days?"

Ellie ran the words through her mind, shutting down, mottling, oxygen deprivation, dehydration. One nurse thought tonight, another, a few days. "They can't say for sure."

"Too bad. I think it would be kind of nice to know. I want to make sure I have my mouth closed."

Ellie laughed again, and then instantly choked up. All the years she wasted, not getting to know her Grandma. "Can I get you anything? Are you comfortable? Are you warm? Are you in pain?"

"I'm fine. Just make sure if I die with my mouth open, you close it quickly. God forbid I look like Jacob Marley. Scrooge..." she said, in her tiny frail little voice, arms out and trembling. "Scrooge...."

Ellie found herself laughing again. "I'll make sure. Don't worry."

"And put my hands like this." She showed her how, nice and dainty-like on her chest. "I want my fingernails to show."

Ellie nodded and said she would, tears springing to her eyes once more.

"I think I'll take a little nap now."

Ellie said that was a good idea, and that she'd take one, too. The limited sleep she'd had in the last forty-eight hours was catching up to her. She propped her feet on the rung of Grandma Betty's bed, and leaned her head on the chair back. When the nurse made her rounds at one in the morning, they were both still asleep.

*   *   *

Two residents died before dawn, but not Grandma Betty. She woke off and on throughout the night, and she and Ellie would talk. Her roommate April woke several times, too, and would ask for water. "Please," she'd say, "just a little water."

Ellie went and asked the nurse if it was okay to give her some. "Sure, if you want. But you don't have to. If you ignore her, she'll go back to sleep. She gets her nights confused with her days."

Ellie gave her water each time. She didn't want much. "Just enough to wet my lips. Thank you."

Come daybreak, the place turned into an anthill; nurses and aides crisscrossing in and out of rooms everywhere. "I can't believe they get people up so early," Ellie commented. "What's the point?"

"The night shift has to have so many of them up and dressed before the day shift."

Poor April; she'd been up and washed and dressed for close to an hour now, and breakfast wasn't for another hour and a half. No coffee, no juice, nothing, just up and dressed and sitting there waiting. "Imagine doing that at home," Grandma Betty said. "Yeah, right."

An orderly entered the room and mopped the floor around them. An overwhelming smell of disinfectant permeated the air.

"You might as well go." Grandma Betty told Ellie. "Ain't nothing happening here."

Ellie hesitated. "I wish there was something I could do."

"There is. You're doing it."

"But surely...."

"No. Now go. Go ride Damian."

Riding Damian *was* her Saturday morning ritual. And always, on the way home, she'd visit her grandmother and tell her all about it.

"Go. As long as I have to be alive, I might as well have something to look forward to."

"But...." She looked so weak.

"No. Now go."

After a shower and change, Ellie arrived at the barn. Abby was waiting for her. "Where have you been? I tried calling and everything."

"Why? What's up?"

"Everything!" She followed Ellie into the tack room. "First of all, Victor claims he caught five crows and they all got away."

"What?"

"Who knows? I think he's lying. He reeks. Anyway, listen. I had a pet psychic do a reading on Bubba, and guess what? He doesn't like the name Bubba."

Ellie looked at her.

"It's true."

Ellie retrieved her saddle and bridle and walked past her.

"You don't believe me, do you?"

"No, I'm just not sure I believe her."

"Why? Wait a minute. How'd you know it was a her?"

"I don't know. Maybe I'm psychic, too."

"Ellie...? What's the matter with you?"

Ellie stopped and looked back at her. "Nothing. I'm just tired. Did you ride Bubba...I mean uh...? What are we calling him now? Did you ride him yet?"

Abby hesitated. "No, I was waiting for you. But never mind. I don't like you anymore," she said, and Ellie couldn't help but laugh.

"All right. So what else did she say?"

"Well." Abby's eyes lit up. "She said he's very sensitive and…. Wait, there she is. Come talk to her. She's doing Jenny's horse next."

Ellie sighed. Of all days. Any other day, but today. "Abby, wait."

Too late. She called the woman over. "This is my friend I was telling you about."

"How nice to meet you."

"You, too." When they shook hands, tiny sparks of electricity sent shocks through both of them. "Sorry," Ellie said, blaming it on static. "It's probably my sweater."

"That's okay. It could have been me."

The two exchanged what could only be described as a deep-rooted glance. Then the woman walked on and Abby turned to Ellie, her voice low. "What was that all about?"

"I don't know. I guess I mirrored her eyes." She was too tired to "keep things to herself " as she'd done all her life, to not talk about it, to hide what she knows, what she senses.

"What? So she's a fake?"

"No, not really. She has some abilities. But she's also sold out."

"What do you mean?

Ellie shrugged. "That a lot of it's for show. It's sad. I think she could help a lot of people."

"How?"

"By telling the truth. Not every horse is going to communicate with her, every dog, every cat, every person." Ellie unlocked her tack trunk and reached inside for her lead shank. "But how much money would that make her?"

"So what are you saying? She lies."

"Lies? No." Ellie hesitated. "Does she tell people what they want to hear? Yes." Ellie looked at her and smiled. "What else she did tell you?"

Abby paused. "About when he dumps me, she said he doesn't like how I use my legs."

"Did she watch you ride?"

"No, but I told her what he does." Abby had taken notes. She handed the paper to Ellie, watched her eyes as she read over it, and waited. "So…?"

Ellie handed them back. "Wrong horse. This would have fit Wendy. She rides like this. You, you're sitting up there half the time just waiting to fall. And do you know how I know - I ride with you! I see you!"

Abby laughed.

"Now come on, are you wanting to ride yet or not?"

"Yes, I told you, I was waiting for you." She followed Ellie into Damian's stall. "So do you think there's any truth to *any* of it?"

Ellie hooked the lead shank onto Damian's halter, gave him a hug, and thought for a moment. "Maybe." She straightened Damian's forelock and looked into his eyes. "Hey, Damian," she said softly. At the sound of his name, he pricked his ears. "Do you like your name, Damian?" He pricked his ears again.

"Wait!" Abby hurried to go try that on Bubba. "Hey, Bubba," she said. He raised his head and looked at her. "Do you like the name Bubba?" Nothing. Not even the blink of an eye.

Ellie watched from between the stall boards.

"Come on, Bubba. Say something."

Again, nothing. He just looked at her. And with that, Abby declared the matter settled. "From this day forward, he shall be called by his registered name, Sir Winston. Sir Winston the Third."

Ellie bowed in his honor.

There were no mishaps today. Both horses worked well. Saturdays were always good ride days, which, as they were cooling out, Ellie started thinking about. "It doesn't make any sense. But then again, maybe it does."

"What do you mean?"

"I don't know. Horses don't know one day from the next, but they do know night from day." She glanced at the rafters, again wondering what it was that day that glistened. Sundown, it's usually sundown when they ride during the week. Perhaps just the right angle of the sun....

After they turned the horses out in the pasture, ever curious, Ellie first checked to see if Victor was around, and then headed for the hayloft. Abby was right behind her. "Do you really think something's spooking him when he does that?"

"Yes," she said. And looked and looked.

They found nothing.

~ 18 ~

When Grandma Betty opened her eyes, there stood Ellie with this rather tall young woman of about the same age at her side. The woman looked vaguely familiar, but she couldn't quite place her.

"Grandma, this is my friend Abby."

"Ah, how nice." Grandma Betty yawned and closed her eyes again.

According to the nurse, Ellie's father and Jewel had just left, and had had a "wonderful visit." Ellie didn't know if she should disturb her; she was resting so comfortably. Another yawn however, and she was wide-awake. "Jewel brought me some more food, Ellie. Your dad looked upset with me when I said I wasn't hungry, so I ate it."

Ellie smiled. She'd probably made Jewel's day. "Uh...." The nurse had also informed Ellie that the room would have to be vacated for two hours while the exterminator sprayed. She relayed the news.

"What?" Grandma Betty was appalled. "For what?"

"Ants. They said it's the time of year for ants, and...."

"You go tell them I said no. Jesus, I'm a dying woman for God's sake! What the hell do I care about ants!"

Ellie laughed, and taking her lead that it was okay, so did Abby.

"They said you could stay in your bed, and that they'll wheel you into the social hall."

"No. Wheel me outside, Ellie. Go see if you can wheel me outside. I don't want to go to that social hall. It ain't social there. Who are they kidding? It's like a morgue."

"All right, I'll go check and see."

With Ellie gone, Grandma Betty turned to Abby for support. "Isn't it Saturday? Why are they doing this on a Saturday?"

Abby shrugged hesitantly. "I don't know. It does seem rather stupid, doesn't it?"

Stupid or not, within a matter of minutes, the exterminators worked their way down the hall and out came April's bed first, then Grandma Betty's with her in it and cussing a blue streak.

"Goddamn sons of bitches! Ellie! Ellie go tell them!"

"I did, Grandma. It's okay. If the door's wide enough, they're going to let us go out into the courtyard."

Sadly, it was not. The door was about two inches too narrow to accommodate a hospital bed, and with Grandma Betty's hopes raised momentarily and then dashed, this called for additional wrath. "Why in the hell would they make a doorway that doesn't fit?"

Army nurse had the answer. "Because it's not a fire escape door. In case of fire, you would not want anyone to exit that way. The courtyard is surrounded by the building. It would mean sure death."

Grandma Betty looked at her. "I'm already a sure death! So what? Push me out there and forget you ever knew me. I ain't going to that social hall. Ellie, tell her. Tell her I ain't going to that social hall."

Ellie laughed. Her amusement at the situation drew a frown from the nurse.

"Maybe we can go out another door?" Abby suggested.

"No, they're all the same to the courtyard."

"What about maintenance? Isn't there a door or a gate they use from the outside for mowing and gardening?" Ellie asked.

The nurse hesitated. "Now that you mention it, yes. There is one. But I don't have time to...."

"I do. We do," Ellie said. "Can we push her out and around and go in that way?" She and Abby instantly flanked both sides, Abby taking her lead again and assuming a ready and efficient stance.

"Please," Grandma Betty pleaded.

"I don't know." The nurse appeared to be mulling it over, mapping it out in her mind. She even would turn and glance in one direction, and then another, as if maneuvering corners. "All right. But no shenanigans. I mean it."

"Shenanigans?" Abby looked at her.

"I'll tell you later," Ellie said, and promised the nurse. "No shenanigans."

Grandma Betty waved to everyone in passing, and once outside, drew a sigh of relief. It would be tempting to die during the day, if it meant never having to go back inside. "Right here," she said. "Under this shade tree. What kind of tree is this anyway?" It had tiny little pods on it.

"I don't know. Something ornamental," Abby guessed.

"Ornamental. I wonder when that all came about?" Grandma Betty reached up to feel one of the pods, touched it gently with her fingertip. It fluttered in the breeze.

Ellie glanced around. A beautiful day and they had the courtyard practically to themselves. All this elaborate landscaping, and but two or three residents out to enjoy it. Abby smiled at the elderly man across the way.

"Afternoon," he said, tipping his hat. "Nice day, eh?"

"What'd he say?" Grandma Betty asked.

"He said it's a nice day," Ellie said.

Grandma Betty agreed. She waved in the man's general direction, the little pods obscuring her view.

"Are you warm enough, Grandma?"

"Oh, yes. Quite. But if you wouldn't mind putting my head down a little. There, that's good." Ellie sat at her one side, Abby the other. "A captive audience," Grandma Betty said, grinning. "Let's see now. What can we talk about?"

Ellie hesitated, at a loss. But as usual, Abby had plenty to say. "I had a psychic reading done on my horse this morning."

"Oh?" Grandma Betty fixed her eyes on the young woman. "Why?"

"Well." Abby told her the whole story. Even the part about Ellie thinking there was something in the hayloft scaring Bubba. "I mean, Sir Winston."

"And you're supposing it's this guy Victor?"

Ellie shrugged. "Yes. Only I can't figure out why. He doesn't dislike Abby. He dislikes me."

"Dislike?" Abby rolled her eyes.

"Oh, Ellie," Grandma Betty said, glancing from one to the other and reading between the lines. "There's nothing more dangerous than a man like that. You be careful around him. Some men are just plain mean and can't take no for an answer. They prey on women, little girls, little boys. They're sick."

Ellie nodded. "Prey, predator," she said, as much to herself as them. "The hawk."

"I say we have Lolita pluck his eyes out," Abby suggested. This, as the Army nurse made an appearance.

"Everything all right?"

"Fine. Everything's fine."

"Good. I'll be leaving shortly and don't want to hear about any trouble."

"Me, too," Grandma Betty said.

The woman just looked at her for a second and then her usual dour face broke into a smile. "Betty, if I'm only half as lively at your age."

Grandma Betty saluted her. "Permission to carry on?"

The nurse chuckled. "Permission to carry on granted."

It wasn't long before Grandma Betty was closing her eyes and dozing off and on. "The air smells so good," she said. "It's wonderful out here. Ahhhh, listen. Isn't that a whippoorwill?"

"I think it is."

"Isn't it cool how birds mate for life," Abby commented.

"I married for life every time," Grandma Betty said. "It was their dying that kept messing things up."

Ellie and Abby chuckled.

"Three husbands and only one child. It weren't for lack of trying though. I loved sex. I always did. At times, I still miss it, you know."

Ellie and Abby laughed, Abby blushing as well.

"I'm sorry, dear. Is this embarrassing you?"

"No, not really. It's just...."

"That it's coming from an old woman. Who better to say? Those teens you see on TV sashaying around? Why, they're just little puppies. They have no idea."

"Amen," Abby said. "I hate that. Just because they're young and skinny and perky and...little!"

Ellie laughed. Grandma Betty had hit on a nerve with Abby, one of her pet peeves. Little women. Considering Abby stood at six-foot-one, most were little to her.

"Just once I'd like to wear pink and ruffles and not feel like a freak. Or look like a freak for that matter either."

"Ruffles?" Ellie said. "I can see the pink, but ruffles?"

Abby smiled. "All right, maybe that was a slight exaggeration. But I feel like Bubba. No wonder he doesn't like being called Bubba. It's like people calling me Stretch. Hey, Stretch. How's the air up there, Stretch? Whatcha see up there, Stretch? Oh, yeah...well stretch this!"

Grandma Betty clapped her hands. "Bravo! Bravo!"

The three of them laughed, and then exhaled a collective sigh. "You know what I'm thinking." Grandma Betty said, glancing around. "I'm thinking if they took more of us out every day like this, just to sit and look around and chat, it wouldn't be such a bad place. When I first came and could walk, I used to come out a lot. Remember?"

Ellie nodded. "That was before the pneumonias," she told Abby, which made no sense to any of them, particularly in light of Grandma Betty's feelings on the subject.

"Fresh air would be the best thing for it. But no, they want you cooped up in your room or in some damned hospital. That may keep you alive, but it ain't living. What point is there in outliving everyone, all cooped up by yourself? Do you know that there's a woman on my floor who hasn't had a visitor in over nine years. Nine years without any family or friends. Can you believe that?"

Abby tried to find the silver lining. "I imagine the staff becomes their family."

"For a while, till they change jobs or quit. They don't come visit then either. The earth is the only constant. The sun, the moon. They're afraid we'll get sunburned. They're afraid we'll get a chill. They're afraid we'll fall."

"But aren't those all legitimate concerns?" Abby asked.

"Yes," Grandma Betty said, sadly. "Ahhhh, life...."

Ellie adjusted the blanket up around her shoulders.

"If just maybe once a week...."

"*Betty.*"

Grandma Betty turned her head, listening.

"What is it, Grandma?"

"*Betty.*"

"Did you hear that? Did someone call me?"

"No."

"You sure?"

Ellie hesitated. "I think so. Why, what did they say?"

"They called my name."

Ellie and Abby exchanged concerned glances.

"Do you want to go back inside?"

"Goodness gracious, no," Grandma Betty said. "Whoever it is will just have to wait. I will not die during the day, and that's all there is to it."

*   *   *

It was a little after four in the afternoon before the residents were allowed back into their rooms. The majority were transported or assisted directly to the dining area, to give the insecticide/pesticide fumes a little longer to dissipate. One of the women still parked in the hallway complained to Ellie and Abby and Grandma Betty as they passed, that the fumes were burning her eyes.

"Oh, no they're not," a nurse at the station scoffed. "It's just your imagination."

Abby felt sorry for the woman. "Gees. Her eyes did look red."

"Who was it?" Grandma Betty asked.

"I don't know. A woman in a wheelchair. Short dark hair, thick glasses."

"Mary. I'll bet it was Mary. That woman's a hypochondriac. She's the one responsible for them not bringing the dog around anymore. Said it gave her fleas and caused a whole big fuss."

Ellie and Abby got Grandma Betty situated, no easy task, since an orderly had already put April's bed back into the room; April's being the one closest to the door. They had to move it one way then another, then another, and another, almost got the bed by, but got totally stuck and had to back out and start all over. Second attempt, they moved Grandma Betty's lounge chair over by April's bed first, the dresser over also. Third attempt, back and forth, back and forth, this time, they got the bed in and up against the wall. Abby pushed the chair back in place.

"Ten-thirty, Grandma?"

Grandma Betty smiled. "Ten-thirty."

Ellie hugged her gently and kissed her on the cheek. It was Abby's turn to say good-bye. She hesitated. She didn't know what to say. Good-bye seemed too casual. "We'll walk the labyrinth for you tomorrow, Betty. And when we get to the center...." Tears welled up in Abby's eyes. "I'll pray for you." She bent down and kissed Grandma Betty on the forehead.

"Wear pink," Grandma Betty said.

Abby promised she would.

No sooner had they gone, Grandma Betty had another visitor. Her doctor.

~ 19 ~

When Ellie arrived home and picked up the phone to dial Diablo, the line was dead. "Wonderful." She plopped down on the couch and leaned her head back and sighed. She should have paid the phone bill yesterday. It was the cutoff date.

Great timing.

She'd so desperately wanted to talk to him, to hear his voice, to thank him for being so kind to her grandmother. To thank him for being there for her as well, for loving her, for her loving him. She wanted to thank him for everything. She laughed at herself. She certainly was in a thankful mood. But then again, why not? She'd had such a wonderful last couple of days with her grandmother. Then there was Diablo finally getting to meet her, before it was too late.

That was a dream come true. As was her and Abby's visit today with Grandma Betty. What a good afternoon they'd shared. She had much to be thankful for.

All except.... She glanced at the clock in the kitchen. It was getting close to the time when she and Abby rode most often on weekdays. She grabbed some carrots and an apple out of the fridge, and headed to the barn. It would be too out of the ordinary for her to ride twice in the same day. It was not standard practice for her or anyone else in the barn for that matter. Victor would notice. Sheila would notice. But if she lucked out and no one was there.... Saturday evenings were usually quiet. Most everyone would have already ridden, or would be away at a show.

She parked near the back of the barn, not visible from the owner's house, and entered by the side door. Damian was standing to the rear of his stall, and as usual, nickered at the sound of her voice. "Hey, big guy." She broke the carrots into pieces and fed them to him one by one, fussing over him and telling him how pretty he was. Then she walked down to check the arena, empty. She wouldn't have to ride, not really, she decided. She could get on him bareback and just walk him around. The setting sun was at just the right angle, shining in on the hayloft through the arena doorway. She put Damian's bridle on him, and led him over to the mounting block. Having had a good day of constant exercise; the ride this morning then turn out in the paddock, he was calm and quiet, even a little lazy actually. "This is nice," she told him, patting his neck. "It wouldn't hurt for you to be like this a little more often."

First time around, nothing. No shiny object, no glimpse of light. Second time around, the same, and the time after that and after that. She gave up after awhile and simply enjoyed the solitary time with Damian. Round and round and round, no change of directions, no smaller circles, just round and round the perimeter, her feet dangling and totally relaxed, and Damian taking deep breaths and sighing every so often. Walking and walking and walking. Horse nirvana; the thought penetrated her mind, a communion. Woman and horse, companion. Mother, father, grandmother...lover. Damian was all she needed at the moment, all she wanted.

Something caught her attention, and she turned, dazed. Victor was standing in the doorway, holding a dead crow and laughing. Laughing like a circus clown, laughing and laughing and laughing. She stared, stared so hard he disappeared. Then he was right in front of her, behind her, in the doorway again, outside on the hill. She opened her eyes with a start, and glanced in all directions. Nothing, alone. She and Damian, totally alone, but for a flash of intense light that came and went. She looked up into the hayloft and saw Victor. This was no dream. He was glaring at her, taunting her, leering, the light blinding, flashing, flashing, flashing....

"Ellie."

She turned, stared again, tried to focus. "Diablo?"

He smiled. "I figured this is where you'd be."

She hesitated, wanting to glance back into the hayloft, but wouldn't, couldn't. She kept her eyes on Diablo, walked Damian up next to him.

"I tried to call you," he said.

"I know, my phone's out. I tried to call you, too."

Damian stood tossing his head, entertaining himself with his mane and forelock whipping up and down.

"There was no answer, it just kept ringing."

Ellie leaned down and kissed him.

"How's your Grandma?"

"She's still with us. She has her heart set on tonight."

Diablo shook his head, still uncomfortable with this concept of looking forward to death. "I figured if I was going to get to see you...."

Ellie slid off Damian and pulled the reins over his head. "What time is it?"

Diablo checked his watch. "Seven-thirty-five." When Damian advanced toward him, Diablo stepped back. "If he comes any closer, I'm going to drop kick him."

Ellie laughed. If only Damian hadn't tried to bite him that one time. "Here," she said, and tossed him the reins. "He'll walk with you, watch."

"No way." Diablo tried handing them back, but when he did, Damian moved closer to him. Out of instinct, Diablo nudged him and was surprised when Damian started walking alongside him. "Ellie, take him."

Ellie laughed. "You'd better not turn him loose. We only have two hours and he'll never let us catch him." Diablo shook his head. "Come on," she said, backing up farther and farther away and leaving them totally on their own. "You can feed him his apple and he'll love you forever."

*   *   *

Ellie arrived at the nursing home at ten-thirty, right on time, fresh out of Diablo's arms and in the mellowest of moods. Grandma Betty's roommate April was sound asleep, Grandma Betty, too. The sight of her sleeping so soundly brought a smile to Ellie's face, until second glance.

There was an IV attached to her grandmother's arm. Dextrose.

Ellie turned on her heels and walked back down the hall to the nurses' station. "Why is she being given fluids?"

"She's dehydrated."

"I don't understand." Ellie stared in frustration. The dehydration was nothing new. "But...."

"I'll be down in a minute. Let me finish this report and I'll be right there."

Ellie walked back to Grandma Betty's room in a fog. This didn't make sense. Surely her grandmother didn't want this? Once again, Ellie struggled with whether or not to wake her.

"Good luck," the nurse said, when she entered the room and Ellie voiced her concerns to the woman. "About an hour after her Kemoran shot, she went out like a light."

"You gave her Kemoran?"

"It was on her chart."

Ellie sat down in the chair and let her arms drop. This was unbelievable, a nightmare. She drew a deep breath, tried calming herself. "You're all supposed to call me before any non-routine medication is administered. She's allergic to Kemoran, remember?"

The nurse glanced at her chart. "Actually she's not exactly allergic to it. According to her records, it just rebounds on her after a while. There's a difference. The doctor prescribed only half her usual dose. She'll be fine."

Ellie stared out the window into the night, close to tears. She wouldn't be fine. She was dying. She was dying tonight, and she was dying drugged. The nurse left the room unnoticed. Ellie dug into her purse for some change and went and phoned her father. Jewel answered.

"They drugged Grandma," Ellie said, her voice cracking. "I can't believe they fucking drugged her. Where's Dad? I need to talk to Dad. Tell him to make them stop. Tell them not to do this to her...." She leaned back against the wall, and slid to the floor, trembling and in tears. "Tell him to make them stop. Please...tell him to make them stop."

Her father came into the room and found Jewel crying. "Who is it?" he asked, and took the phone. "Who is this?"

Ellie sobbed into the phone. "It's me. They...."

"Ellie? What's wrong?"

Ellie wept uncontrollably. "They...." She wiped her eyes and tried to catch her breath. "They gave Grandma Kemoran. They gave her Kemoran."

"She was in pain, Ellie. What did you want them to do? She requested it."

"No, she didn't. She wouldn't. She knew I'd be back. I told her I'd be back."

"Ellie. Ellie, listen to me."

"No. You probably told them it was okay."

"Ellie...."

"No." She dropped the phone and buried her head in her hands. "She wouldn't do this to me. I know my Grandma. She wouldn't do this to me."

~ 20 ~

It was almost three in the morning before Grandma Betty stirred, and then only to cry out, frightened and confused. "I'm right here, Grandma," Ellie said, holding her hand. "I'm right here. You're okay."

"But I had my check! I know I had my check! What could have happened to it? I have no money now! What will I do?"

"It's okay. It's okay."

"But I have to find it! Don't you understand? I have to find it!"

Ellie glanced frantically around the room, saw a pile of napkins on the table and grabbed one and put it in Grandma Betty's hand. "Here, I found it. Here it is, Grandma."

"Oh thank heaven. How would I have paid my bills? I'm on social security!"

"Yes, I know. Everything's okay now. Here, let me put it away for you."

Grandma Betty relinquished the napkin and closed her eyes. "Put it in a safe place, Ellie. Please."

"I will." Ellie went through the motions of pretending to hide her grandmother's check in the top dresser drawer. Awakened by the fuss, April asked if she could have a drink of water.

"Of course." Ellie walked over and held the cup to her mouth, one of those "sippy cups" that toddlers use.

"Thank you," April said, her quivering hands wrapped around Ellie's. "Thank you so much."

"You're welcome." Ellie smiled, touched and yet saddened at the same time by this formality of politeness, and gently fixed her blanket. When she sat back down in her grandmother's chair, the room fell silent again. "As still as a mouse. As still as a house." Ellie couldn't remember the nursery rhyme. Was it a rhyme or a song? "When all through the house...." Words and phrases tumbled through her mind. "Tea for two, and you and you. Remember, re-mem-a-member, re-member...." She listened to her grandmother's breathing, listened to April's breathing, listened to her own breathing. They were all three breathing as one, in perfect harmony, perfect rhythm.

"Re-mem-ber. Re-mem-a-member. Re-member." Ellie tried to get the words of that song to stop invading her mind, to leave her alone, to go elsewhere. But it just kept coming back, crowding the silence, crowding the breathing.

When an aide checked in on them, Ellie welcomed the intrusion. "Would you mind staying with my Grandma a few minutes?" she whispered. "I need to go to the ladies room."

"Sure, no problem. Go ahead, I could use a break."

As Ellie walked down the hall, the shuffle from her shoes on the linoleum was the only sound she heard. The woman's comment had both saddened and touched her as well. To think of sitting with a dying resident, as "taking a break." Sitting down on the job, so to speak. And yet, how many patients and residents had this woman cared for and watched die, dressed for the undertaker, closed their eyes, combed their hair.

Ellie washed her face and hands in the stillness of the ladies room, feeling alien, detached, observing her every move as if a stranger from a distance. A cloudy distance. She looked in the mirror, and something about the way she looked in the mirror reminded her of her Grandma. Same expression, same furrow in her brow.

"I am never wearing red," she told herself. And laughed at the thought of telling her grandmother that. If only she would wake, one last time, and understand. Understand that although the two of them were alike in many ways, Grandma Betty was one of a kind.

"Betty Boop." Ellie chuckled. "Tell me about the time you dressed up like Betty Boop, Grandma. Tell me."

"Well, dear. It was a fundraiser. The roof on the Legion was leaking and could no longer be patched, and...."

A nurse entered the ladies room, scattering Ellie's thoughts. The woman had blood all over her uniform. "A resident fell and broke his nose," she said. "What a night!"

*   *   *

Grandma Betty woke again a little after five, groggy, but rather coherent. "Oh, Ellie. Thank heaven you're here. Could you go see if I'm due for another pain shot?"

Ellie stared, reality sinking in. So she did ask for the Kemoran, after all. "Grandma, if you have one, it will only put you back to sleep. Is that what you want?"

"I'll be all right. It won't make me sleepy."

"It will, Grandma. It always does," Ellie said, not bothering to mention all the other side effects that had already begun to manifest.

"But the doctor said. He said he'd tell the nurses I could have it if I'm in pain."

"Are you in pain, Grandma?"

"Well, yes."

"Now?"

"Not so much, but it may get worse. It probably will get worse."

"Could I have a drink, please?" April asked.

Ellie walked around to the other side of April's bed.

"Ellie?"

"I'm right here, Grandma."

"Did you go ask?"

"No, I'm giving April a drink of water." Oh God, she thought, it's sounds like I'm watering a horse. "I'm over here with April. I'll be right there."

In the short time it took for Ellie to come back around to her grandmother's side, Grandma Betty became agitated. "I don't understand why you don't want me to have it."

Ellie hesitated. This was ludicrous. This was ridiculous. This was Kemoran. "Grandma, can I see if there's something else they can give you? Something maybe even better."

When Grandma Betty agreed, Ellie headed down the hall to the nurses' station, mumbling to herself. "You're a junkie, Grandma. An eighty-five-year-old junkie." She looked up to see her father walking toward her.

"Dad, why are you here?" It wasn't even daybreak.

"I was worried about you."

"You shouldn't be. I'm fine." She turned to the nurse and started to ask about the medication. Her dad interrupted. "Dad, please," she said. "*I* need to handle this, not you. Okay? I just want to ask if there's something else she can be given. Extra-strength Tylenol, for Christ sake, if nothing else."

The nurse paused. "I won't be able to get a hold of the doctor for another hour or so."

"What about that stuff she got when she had the toothache?"

The nurse flipped back through the chart, glanced at the calendar, and shrugged, but in a positive way. "It'd be a stretch, but the time on the prescription's still good."

"It's non-narcotic, right?"

"Yes."

"What is it?" her father asked.

"Avimex," the nurse said. "It's not quite as strong as Kemoran, but it will numb the pain."

Her dad shifted his weight. "Are there any side effects?"

Ellie looked at him, just looked at him a second, and wanted to scream. Instead, she calmly rattled off the side effects, amazing herself, even as the words were coming out of her mouth. She couldn't remember the name of the medication, but could damned well tell you the side effects.

"Liver damage?" her father repeated, top of the list.

"Yes, liver damage, with long-term use. Only she's not going to be here tomorrow, Dad, soooo...."

Her father took a step back, conceding, and walked with Ellie down the hall. "Here," he said, handing her a bag. She took it from him and opening it, swallowed hard. Hot chocolate and a cinnamon fried cake, her favorite breakfast ever since high school. Her bottom lip started trembling.

"It's all right," he said, putting his arms around her. "It's all right. If she wants to die, I'll let her die. Okay? I won't interfere."

Ellie nodded, snug in his embrace. "I love you, Dad."

"I love you too, Kitten."

Kitten. It was the nickname he'd given her as a child when she fell out of the tree that day and didn't get hurt. It had been years since he called her that. She was a woman now, he'd said, and you don't call your daughter a cat.

"Thanks, Dad." She wiped her eyes and the two of them entered Grandma Betty's room together.

~ 21 ~

Abby answered the door and was surprised to find Ellie standing there. She was early, two hours early. "That's why I stopped by. I don't want to go." They were supposed to walk a labyrinth this afternoon. "I'm really not in the right frame of mind. I just didn't want you freaking out when I didn't show."

"But why? We promised Grandma Betty."

"No, *you* promised her."

Abby stared. "Is she...?"

"No, she's still with us." Ellie explained the situation and turned to leave.

"Ellie, come on. I need to go."

"Then go. You don't need me."

"Yes I do."

Ellie sighed. "It's no big deal, I'm sure, really. It's a canvas with a maze painted on it, and you walk around and...."

"It's not a maze. It's a labyrinth."

"Whatever. Like I said, it's no big deal."

"But it is. Something's going to happen today. I can feel it. We're supposed to go, you and me. We were meant to go. We have to go."

Ellie hesitated and shook her head. "You said this about the cornucopia, you know."

"Yeah, but that was different. I didn't know then what I know now."

Ellie smiled faintly. "Oh?"

"I can't put it into words. But I was thinking maybe after we walk the labyrinth...." She picked up the brochure. "Here. Look, you're supposed to concentrate on something pressing, some issue you're dealing with, and while you walk the labyrinth, think about it. This one woman suggests you even say the problem over and over in your mind while you're walking."

"See, that's what bothers me with all these things. What if you don't have a problem? Problems you can do anything about that is?"

"Then you walk in peace."

"I can walk in the woods."

"You can also walk the labyrinth. Come on, come in the kitchen," Abby said. "Michael's cooking sushi."

"*Cooking* sushi?"

"Yes, we don't like it raw. He calls it san-sushi! It's really tasty!"

"What happened to vegetarianism?" Ellie asked, trailing behind reluctantly.

"We're compromising. We only eat meat or fish on weekends."

* * *

Abby dressed in pink: pink sweater, pink slacks, pink scarf. She gazed at herself in the mirror. "I look like a guy in drag."

Ellie laughed. "No, you don't. You look pretty."

"Yeah, right." Abby tucked her stomach in, turned one way and then the other. "You sure?"

Ellie nodded. "Lose the scarf."

The labyrinth walk was being held at a local conservatory. The parking lot was packed; in its center, lay the labyrinth. Ellie got out of the car, shaking her head. Her comment that it was a piece of canvas with a maze painted on it wasn't far off.

An explanation of the labyrinth's origin was in progress. "Ancient times...healing properties...insightful."

Ellie stared. All she saw was canvas and paint.

"And now I would like to introduce...."

Abby nudged her. It was the "flower-child woman."

"Each one of you will experience something different as you walk the labyrinth. No two experiences are alike, just as no two people are alike. Some will feel elation, some a sense of calm. To some, this could be a life-altering occurrence. To others, just a walk in the park or the woods."

Ellie glanced away; was it her imagination the woman's eyes seemed to rest on her with that last statement?

"As in life, as you walk through the labyrinth, you will follow strangers...friends...and family. You will walk in their footsteps, and in the footsteps of those before them. On your way out, some you will pass, some will pass by you. Some you will acknowledge; a smile, a nod, an embrace. Some you will choose to ignore. You are all on the same path, and yet alone on your own journey. Allow those before you, time. Be mindful of those that follow. And in the center, know you are not lost...as to come into the center, is to begin your way back out. There are no false paths; there are no dead ends. This is not a puzzle; this is not a maze. It is a circle of wonder and reflection. Walk in spirit, go in peace."

One by one, the assembled took off their shoes and stepped onto the labyrinth. Some were eager to go first, some held back. Abby suggested she and Ellie walk well apart, so as not to be distracted by one another.

"Whatever," Ellie said.

Abby looked at her. "If you say that one more time, I'm gonna scream."

Ellie chuckled. This was silly. A crowd of people walking around a parking lot on a canvas in their bare feet or socks. What glorious thing was supposed to come from that? They'd be better off going over and sitting down under a tree.

Flower-child woman, who had been milling about, appeared at her side. "Do you have any idea how far along you'd be," she said, "if you'd only just once start out with an open mind?"

Ellie smiled politely.

Abby stepped onto the labyrinth next, all eager, and pink socks. An elderly woman followed, her feet twisted and gnarled, and after her; a man with snow white hair, then a teenage girl.

Ellie glanced over her shoulder at a flock of crows circling the conservatory, and high above them, a buzzard. She squinted in the sunlight. Waiting to pick my bones, no doubt, she thought.

Flower-child woman took Ellie by the hand, waited for her to step out of her shoes, and led her to the labyrinth. "Walk in spirit."

Ellie relinquished the security of her hand, and was on her own. One foot on the canvas, and a myriad of emotions washed over her. Sadness, a tremendous sadness, then embarrassment, don't be seen crying, fear, of what? Happiness, remorse. She reasoned herself through each one, step by step. This was not the time and place to become emotional. She forced her thoughts elsewhere, recalling bits and pieces of what Abby had said. Bring a problem, bring a concern, meditate, rejoice. That had a nice ring to it, a nice sound. Bring a problem, bring a concern, meditate, rejoice. She imagined saying it out loud, a mantra. She imagined her voice low, she imagined it high. She imagined putting it to music - she imagined it being read. Bring a problem, bring a concern, meditate, rejoice.

The flock of crows landed amidst the hostas, the buzzard still soaring overhead.

Victor. His name invaded Ellie's thoughts, her being. His name, his sound, his scent, his presence. Victor. She glanced ahead for Abby. There were people sitting in the center of the labyrinth; a woman, arms folded and in tears, another with hands pressed gently to the canvas, a man with palms raised to the sky. Abby entered and immediately knelt to the ground.

The threat was not going to go away. The threat was real. Ellie concentrated on putting one foot in front of the other. She'd done nothing to entice Victor, nothing to provoke him. How infuriating to have to think of that man, to have him constantly invade her thoughts. How infuriating to have to deal with him at all. Victor. Ignore him, a voice in her mind said. But how could she? Look where ignoring him had gotten her. He was frightening the horses. He was building a cage. He was stalking her. He knew she'd be back the other night to check on Damian. He'd been waiting for her....

The crows took flight, a chorus of whispering wings as they landed in the treetops.

Ellie squared her shoulders, determined. No longer would she ignore Victor. Instead, she was going to confront him. She remembered a saying she'd heard years ago, "If I don't have a problem with you, and you have a problem with me, then it's not my problem." But it *was* her problem.

Abby rose from her knees, radiant.

The elderly woman entered then, followed by the man with the snow-white hair, the teenager. And then Ellie. She had no expectations. It was just the center, a little round circle on a canvas. Nothing had happened so far. Nothing was going to happen. She stood, staring at the pattern. She just stared. And as she stared, a feeling of warmth came over her. She had no desire to sit, or kneel, to touch the canvas. She just stood there, feeling warm, feeling safe. All around her, people were walking the same path, each bringing their own problems and concerns, their own celebrations...and for the first time in her life, she didn't mind not being alone. She *wasn't* alone.

Leaving the center, she thought of Grandma Betty. She thought of her with every step thereafter, winding in and out, round and round. She thought of her father and Jewel. She thought of Diablo. She thought about her life, Grandma Betty's life. She thought about death. "Scrooge..." she could hear Grandma Betty saying. "This is Jacob Marley." She smiled; she couldn't stop smiling. All she wanted to do was smile. At the end waiting for her, were Abby and flower-child woman, smiling as well.

~ 22 ~

Ellie phoned the nursing home to check on Grandma Betty, was told she was sleeping comfortably, and drove to the barn to confront Victor. Abby wasn't so sure this was a good idea.

"What if he's not in a good mood?"

"Too bad."

"But?"

Ellie smiled reassuringly. "I'm just going to talk to him. This can't go on. It's gone on long enough."

"Maybe we should go talk to Sheila."

"And tell her what?"

Abby hesitated. "I don't know. I wish we had proof."

"Well, we don't. And that's why I can't go to her. Victor won't need proof. He knows he's guilty. He knows what he's been doing. He's doing it on purpose."

The two of them got out of the car and walked into the barn. Victor was nowhere to be found. "Do you want me to check up at the house?"

Ellie shook her head. "I'll come back later."

"By yourself? No way. Maybe you should bring Diablo with you."

"Are you kidding? I don't want him to even know. This is my problem, not his. I'll deal with it."

Damian nickered at the sound of Ellie's voice. "Hey, big guy," she said, opening his stall door. "How ya doing?"

Damian walked to the front of the stall and nosed around for a carrot.

"Do you have any treats?" she called to Abby.

"Yes, just a second. Does Damian have water?"

Ellie stepped back to look. "No." His water bucket was empty.

Bubba's, too. Not low. Empty. Abby checked the next stall. The buckets on both sides were full. "Now what are the odds...?" They checked each and every stall down the aisle; all had water. The only two empty were Bubba's and Damian's. "I really, *really* hate that man."

Ellie was already headed for the house.

The farm owner, Sheila, answered the door. "Hi! What's up?"

"Is Victor home?"

"Yeah, he's in the basement. Why?"

"We need to talk to him," Abby said.

"About what?" the woman asked, eyeing Abby up and down, dressed in pink.

"About not watering our horses. All the other horses have water but ours," Ellie said, realizing how ridiculous she probably sounded, even as she said it.

"Maybe they drank it all."

"No, more than likely Victor didn't...."

Ellie touched Abby's arm. "Could you just tell Victor we'd like to talk to him, please."

Sheila hesitated. "Is this about him building the cage for the crows? We can't have them around, Ellie. They're dangerous."

"No, they're not. But that's not what this is about."

"Well, I'll tell him. How long are you going to be here?"

Ellie glanced at her watch. "Not long, ten minutes or so." She'd told the nursing home she'd be there within the hour, should Grandma Betty wake and ask.

"Fine, I'll have him come down to the barn."

No need. Victor appeared at her side. "What's the problem, babe?"

Sheila turned. "They're worried you didn't water their horses."

"What? Why wouldn't I water their horses?" he asked innocently.

The woman looked at Ellie and Abby.

What could they say?

"Well, we just wanted to make sure." Abby stood her ground, even when Ellie nudged her again to go. "We were hoping it wasn't intentional or anything."

"Not hardly," Victor said. "When I washed all the buckets this afternoon, maybe I just forgot to fill those two."

Ellie nodded, backing up, hoping he'd follow them. "Are you going to come down and water them now?"

Victor shrugged. "You two can water them, go ahead." He shut the door on that, but not before both Abby and Ellie distinctly heard him say to Sheila, "What pains in the ass."

"Us?" Ellie glared at the closed door.

"Come on," Abby said. "You were right. She wouldn't believe us anyway."

They walked back to the barn, watered their horses, gave them carrots, and were getting ready to leave, when Ellie decided to go investigate the birdcage. She hadn't wanted to be caught back there before, but with Victor up at the house at the moment, curiosity got the best of her. She rounded the corner of the tool shed, Abby right on her heels, and stopped dead.

The birdcage was huge, looked like a chicken coop, door open, and had bait inside; an injured crow. Ellie approached slowly, not wanting to frighten it, its battered and bloodied wings beating helplessly against its sides.

"Oh dear God," Abby said. "Is it...?"

Ellie shook her head. Victor had tied its feet to the bottom of the coop with wire, the one leg practically severed from its frantic struggle to get free.

"It's okay.... It's okay...." Ellie said softly. She reached underneath the cage, untied its legs, and when it tried desperately to fly but couldn't, caught it and brought it to her chest. "You're okay," she said. "No more harm will come to you. No more harm." With a trembling hand around its neck and a snap of her wrist, she ended the bird's suffering.

Abby stood at her side, with tears in her eyes. "Should we bury it?"

"No." Ellie laid the crow in the field and wiped the blood from her hands onto the grass all around it.

Victor was standing on the front porch of the farmhouse as they pulled out, as if posing for a magazine, one foot on the railing and elbow on knee. Ellie turned when a glint of light caught her eye; the sun reflecting off his cigarette lighter. Flashing, flashing, flashing....

*　　*　　*

Grandma Betty woke with a bad taste in her mouth and numbness in her hands and feet. "Leave it to me to die in bits and pieces," she told Ellie, with a frail laugh. "I wonder what'll go next?"

Ellie smiled. "Can I get you anything? Are you warm enough?"

"I'm fine." She'd been sleeping comfortably off and on since Ellie returned. "I'm sorry I'm not better company."

"You're perfect company, Grandma. Go back to sleep if you want."

"No, that's okay. There's something I want to tell you. It's about Dutch."

Ellie smiled. Dutch was her favorite of the Grandpas she'd had because of Grandma Betty.

"He was a lot like your Diablo."

"How so?" Ellie asked, taking note. That was the first time she hadn't referred to him as the Dildo.

"Oh, he was a lover. He was physical and made everything right that way. But he also used to break my heart. I couldn't trust him, Ellie. Do you trust Diablo?"

Ellie hesitated, taken off guard.

"If ever there was a look worth a thousand words," Grandma Betty said, sadly.

"No, it's not that I don't trust him. I just don't know."

Grandma Betty shook her head. "Dutch would lie about everything. I loved him, but I couldn't believe a word he said. To the day he died, I didn't trust him."

Ellie lowered her eyes to the floor, kept her tongue. Diablo is not Dutch, she wanted to say. Don't judge one by the other. But to declare that, would be disrespectful, particularly under the circumstances. Her grandmother was dying, little by little, as she had just joked, but it was true. Ellie could see it. She could feel it, sense it. At the same time though, she was also going to die and would never know....

"They're two different people, Grandma? They're...." Ellie sat back. Grandma Betty had drifted off to sleep. "Diablo is not Dutch." Ellie said, as much to herself as to the walls. "I do trust him. It's me I can't trust. I'm different."

"You're special," Grandma Betty said, apparently still awake.

Ellie chuckled. "So are you, Grandma. I love you."

"I love you too, dear. Now go on. Go, so you can get back before dark."

Ellie drove straight to Diablo's. She'd originally intended to swing by her apartment and change clothes. The front of her shirt was spattered with crow's blood. She'd planned to stop by the barn next. Victor would be feeding; she could confront him. Diablo wasn't expecting her until much later. She knocked on his door and stood waiting. His car was home, the Harley, home. She knocked again, and held her breath when she heard him yell, "Just a minute!"

He answered the door, hair all mussed, and in nothing but a pair of jeans.

"I'm early," she said, and walked past him, peeling off her shirt even before he'd gotten the door closed. "Sorry I didn't phone. I don't have much time."

Diablo asked about Grandma Betty, asked about the blood on her shirt. Her answer was the same for both. "Later."

*　　*　　*

Grandma Betty had several surprise visits while Ellie was gone. First, her sister Janie. "I haven't seen you in so long. Where have you been?"

"Right here," Janie said. "I've died and gone to heaven. Remember?"

Grandma Betty laughed. Surely she must be dreaming. Janie, in heaven?

A nurse poked her arm with a needle.

"Do you remember the day we skipped school and walked to the movie house?"

"Remember it? It was my idea."

"Yeah, well, I never forgave you for lying to Mommy and Daddy about it."

"Betty, hold your arm still. Lucy, come here and hold her arm down."

Lucy? Grandma Betty tried to open her eyes. They wouldn't budge. "Who the hell is Lucy?"

"Is she that skinny girl from over on Walnut Ridge?"

"No, that was Mary Lou. You're thinking about the Gibson girl."

"Yes, that's her. Lord, was she skinny. I wonder what ever happened to her?"

"I think she ran away from home."

"Oh, that's right. She did. Remember that time she came to school all beat up?"

Grandma Betty shuddered. "Don't talk about that. The last thing I want to talk about while dying is some poor girl getting beat up by her dad."

"I heard she stabbed him."

"When? That day?"

"No, later. Three times in the chest. I heard they buried him with the knife still stuck in his chest."

Grandma Betty tried opening her eyes again. This time they cooperated. "Mercy," she said, glancing around the room. "April? April, are you over there?" She stared at the drawn curtain, wondered if she had the strength to lean over and pull it open. "Janie? Janie, are you still here? Look and see if Lucy's in her bed. Damn, I'm so confused. Where's Ellie?"

"She'll be back in a little while," the nurse said. "Now rest your arm. If you keep moving around so much, it's only going to hurt more."

Grandma Betty focused on the woman. She had big, big eyes. Really big eyes.

"Stop that!"

Grandma Betty jumped. The woman's nose was right in front of hers. "No damned wonder your eyes are so big. Get away! Please," she remembered to add. The woman was gone.

"Hey, Betty!"

Grandma Betty froze. "Dutch...?"

"How you doin'? You okay?"

"Fine, Dutch. How are you? Come here, let me see you?" Grandma Betty searched her mind, searched her eyes, searched inside, searched everywhere. "Dutch? Dutch, where did you go?"

"I'm right here. Look, I'm right here. Smile if you see me."

Grandma Betty smiled.

"You're smiling in the wrong direction, Betty. I'm over here."

Grandma Betty laughed. "Where? Never mind, I don't care. I can hear you. That's enough."

"How are you feeling?"

"All right. It's good to hear your voice."

"Betty…."

Grandma Betty turned. "Who's that?"

"It's me, Sophie. I need to change your diaper, only don't move that arm. Okay?"

"No," Grandma Betty said. "Not now, not while Dutch is here."

"Dutch? Dutch, who?"

"Dutch, my husband. He's here and I don't want him to see me like this. Leave me alone. Please, just leave me alone."

"I'm sorry, Betty, I can't. There's nobody here but you and me. Don't worry, nobody's going to see you. I got the curtain pulled."

"But Dutch was here, I heard him. I heard him! I could even almost see him."

"Betty, you're just going to have to calm yourself down. You hungry, hon? Do you want something to eat?"

"No, I don't eat anymore."

"Oh, is that why they have you on the IV?"

"I guess so," Grandma Betty said, tears welling up in her eyes. "How's come you don't know I don't eat anymore. How is it you don't know?"

"I'm sorry, Betty. I'm new here. Don't cry. I didn't mean to make you cry."

"It's not you…." Grandma Betty wiped her eyes; salty tears trickling down her cheeks. "I'm just so tired, that's all. Is it dark out yet?"

"No, not yet. A little while longer."

Grandma Betty nodded. In a little while, it would all be over.

"Keep that arm still now, okay?"

Grandma Betty folded her hands across her chest, red fingernails showing, and clenched her jaw, just in case. An odd sensation, she thought, this dying. She hoped Ellie got back in time. Being alone was frightening. "April? April, are you there?"

Silence....

~ 23 ~

Diablo wrapped his arms around Ellie and didn't want to let her go. "Why do you have to leave so early? Did you even eat? Why don't we go get something to eat?"

Ellie smiled. This was new, his worried about her eating. "I'm fine."

"No, you're not. You look like hell."

"Thank you."

Diablo shrugged. "Who else'll tell you, if not me?"

Her Grandma, she thought, and fought back instant tears. "I ate at Abby's earlier, I'm fine. Honest."

"What? Lunch?"

"Yes."

"Come on. We can at least go get something at the deli. It won't take long."

Ellie followed him in her car to save time. As soon as she was done eating, she was going to head for the barn. It would still be light out. Sunday evenings were usually pretty active; other people would be there. She glanced at her watch and reached for the menu.

"Ellie...."

She looked up.

"I understand," Diablo said. "A little I mean, about your Grandma."

Ellie searched his eyes.

"I'm proud of you. Okay?"

Ellie nodded, again fighting back tears. "Okay."

Her hands trembled as she ate. She'd said she wasn't hungry, and yet practically wolfed her food down. She talked incessantly. She told him all about the labyrinth.

"I don't get it," he said. "You just walk around this canvas."

"Yes. But not all of them are canvas. Most in fact are made of stone or brick, and are permanent somewhere. Some are in grass. They had pictures of one in a field. It was awesome. And something does happen, Diablo. I can't explain it, but a feeling comes over you."

Diablo smiled. "I'll take your word for it."

Ellie finished eating, kissed and hugged him and left. Eight-thirty-five, she still had some daylight. If she hurried....

She took a shortcut, but caught every light. When she arrived, there were only two cars parked at the barn. One she recognized as belonging to one of the racetrack people. She parked next to it, hesitated, and drew a deep breath. This was the right thing to do, she told herself. Confront Victor now and get it over with. She should have done it long before this. "I can't let it go another day."

When she opened the door and got out of the car, a faint caw sounded in the distance.

She turned, heard it again, and started running. The birdcage. She scrambled over the paddock fence, ran down the hill and around the shed, and screamed as she got close.

Lolita! She was trapped!

Ellie rushed to the cage.

It was padlocked!

"Hold on, hold on...." Lolita frantically beat her wings and head against the sides. "Hold on!" Ellie looked around for something to break the lock. Nothing. She tried stretching the wire mesh, tried pulling it apart, but it sliced her hands. "Damn!" She ran around to the front of the shed, looked inside, and finding a piece of 2x4 with nails pounded into it, grabbed it and ran back and tore away at the wire.

"It's all right. It's all right," she kept saying to Lolita, her voice as calm as she could manage. "I'll get you out. It's all right." She pounded and pounded against the wire. One part let loose. She tried peeling it back, but again, it sliced her hands. More pounding, harder and harder. Finally, the nails in the board tore away a large enough opening. She threw the 2x4 down and eased her arms inside, the jagged wire tearing her flesh. "Come," she said. "Come...."

Lolita held back, her chest heaving, her wings battered and torn. "Come." Too frightened to respond, when she tried to fly again, Ellie grabbed her and very carefully, slowly, eased her arms back out. "It's okay. It's okay. You're free. It's okay." She examined Lolita's head for injury, her body, her legs - Lolita's trusting gaze piercing her heart, her soul. "Damn him!" Ellie glanced toward the field, the place she'd laid the dead crow; spread its blood in a circle...a warning...a threat.

"Damn you!" She called out Victor's name, and turned, raising Lolita to the sky. "You should have paid heed, Victor! You should have listened!"

Clutching Lolita to her chest, time running out, she spit into her hand, again and again, each time draining herself of more and more energy, and forced Lolita to drink. "Drink...." Lolita gulped down the nourishment, her heart beating hard and labored. She drank and drank, until Ellie had nothing left to give. Her side aching, head throbbing, Ellie climbed the hill to the car, barely able to catch her breath, and opened the trunk to get Damian's blanket. She shook it out, placed it on the back seat and laid Lolita on her side and wrapped her tightly. She'd be unable to move, but safe from further injury. She'd have to be examined more carefully, see if she'd broken a wing. God forbid, if she'd broken both. But first, fearing more for Damian now, Ellie started into the barn and thinking twice, ran back around to the birdcage and picked up the 2x4 that had the nails in it. As she started back up the hill, something shiny in the cage caught her eye. A locket. One she knew well. It had belonged to her mother.

She retrieved it, shoved it into her pocket, and hurried to the barn. Bubba was standing in the back of his stall. He appeared to be fine. So did Damian. Ellie opened his stall door, checked his water, his feed tub, checked him. Then she went in search of Victor. The racetrack people said they hadn't seen him. The other boarder there hadn't seen him either. She searched the feed room, tack room, the hayloft, everywhere imaginable, and found herself back at Damian's stall, even angrier. She glanced at her watch. She was going to have to leave. Grandma Betty was expecting her. She leaned against Damian, breathed in his scent, tried calming herself. And turned at the sound of Victor's voice.

"You looking for me?"

She backed up, glaring. "I want this to stop, Victor. Do you understand? I don't know what your problem is, or what's going on with you and this thing you have with me...."

"I don't have a thing with you. I don't know what you're talking about. I don't even like you. I don't like your horse. I don't like your friend."

"Nobody says you have to like us. Just leave us alone. We've done nothing to you."

"That's what you think, all high and mighty."

Damian tossed his head and began fidgeting.

"I see you found your bird."

Ellie glanced at the 2x4, a little more than arm's length away. "How'd you get my locket?"

"Maybe if you'd come home at night, you'd find out."

Ellie moved toward Damian, pretending to attempt to settle him down. Just a little closer and she could reach the 2x4.

"You must not get many phone calls."

Ellie hesitated. Damian started dancing back and forth, blocking her way. "Just leave us alone, okay?"

"I can't," Victor said, stepping inside the stall. "You and I both know that's not what you really want."

"It is," Ellie said. "I don't want anything to do with you. Now please..." Timing Damian perfectly, when he stepped back, tossing his head, she lunged for the 2x4 and turned, only to have Victor snatch it out of her hands. And with that, Damian started bouncing off the walls.

"Oh my God!" Ellie gasped, suddenly realizing the source of Damian's puncture wounds.

"I'm going to teach you how to behave yet!" Victor shouted. And when he raised the 2x4, Damian swung around and started kicking! The first two kicks missed, the succession that followed didn't.

Ellie dropped to the ground and rolled out of the stall fast, then stumbled to her feet amidst a small crowd quickly approaching.

"Easy now..." she heard someone saying. "Easy now...."

"Easy...."

Victor lay in a heap. Damian had stopped kicking, but was repeatedly stepping on him, still trying to get away from him. Sheila, the farm owner attempted to get close to Damian, but he wouldn't have any part of it. "Ellie!" she urged. "Ellie, come help me! Come help me!"

Ellie grabbed his halter and went back into the stall, lunged one way and then the other, to try and stop him. He stepped on Victor yet again. Finally, she got the halter on him and led him out - Damian dancing up and down and snorting and almost getting loose.

"Get me his shank," she said to Diablo, and froze for a split second. Diablo?

A shank. Fortunately she'd pointed to it. He had no idea what a shank was. He grabbed it and started toward her. "Toss it to me," she said. "Slow."

He tossed it to her carefully, then glanced back in the stall, assessed the man's injuries, and took out his cell phone and dialed 911.

Ellie disappeared for a moment, walking Damian in the arena, trying to settle him down, talking to him. He kicked and bucked and squealed over and over. "It's okay," she kept telling him. "It wasn't your fault. It wasn't your fault." But he was too wound up. She gave up and turned him loose in the arena, let him run and run and run, and walked to the stall, dreading what she would find.

"Is he...?" Surely Victor had to be dead.

"No," Diablo said. "All fucked up, but not dead."

A siren sounded, louder and louder, and then went silent as the ambulance turned in off the road.

Ellie looked into the stall. Sheila was bent over Victor, sobbing. Ellie imagined her turning on her, blaming Damian, blaming the crows, blaming her.

"Sheila...?"

The woman shook her head, cradling Victor in her arms. "I'm so sorry, Ellie. I should have known." He was still holding on to the 2x4.

Tears sprang to Ellie's eyes.

Everyone gathered stepped back then as the ambulance crew wheeled a stretcher in and started attending to Victor. "Ma'am," the one said, pulling Sheila off of him. "Ma'am, please."

"Ellie." Diablo reached for her hand. "We have to go."

"What?" Ellie stared at him.

"It's your Grandma. She's dying."

"Oh my God."

"Come on."

<h1 style="text-align:center">~ 24 ~</h1>

In Diablo's family, it was bad luck for a bird to fly into one's house. Having one in a car seemed ten times worse. "Oh, the things I do for you, Ellie," he said, and it made her smile. A sad smile, but a smile nonetheless.

She held Lolita in her lap, still wrapped in Damian's blanket, hesitant to look, to see if she would live or die. There was no time to check her at the barn, no time to.... She'd hardly spoke except to give Diablo directions. It was nightfall.

Diablo explained how he'd phoned the nursing home, worried about her, how they said she hadn't arrived, and that he became even more concerned then, uneasy. When the nurse gave him the news about Grandma Betty failing fast, he told the woman he'd find Ellie and get there as soon as possible. The barn was the only other place he could think she'd be, and arrived just as two women came running out of the house. Apparently, one of the racetrackers, alarmed by the cuts and scratches on Ellie's hands and arms, not to mention her searching for Victor with the 2x4 in her hand, went up to the house and alerted the owner.

"Do you want me to phone the nursing home and find out if…?"

Ellie shook her head. "She'll still be alive. I know it."

Diablo glanced out his side window, hoping for her sake she was right. "You okay?"

She nodded. She'd cleaned her cuts and scratches as best she could, by wiping them on the blanket. She was numb to the pain. Another ten minutes or so, and they'd be there. When Lolita let out a shrill caw, Diablo jumped.

"Jesus Christ!"

Ellie chuckled somewhat at his reaction, and cradled her in her arms, talked to her, hummed to her, pressed her cheek against her small face. She'd put it off long enough; she had to examine her wings. She unwrapped her gently, right wing first, and examined each feather. The tips of three were gone; all were somewhat furled and frayed, but no feathers broken, no broken bones. Left wing, a feather was missing and another barely attached.

Diablo leaned further and further away from them, as far as he could. "Can she fly like that?"

"I don't know. I think so."

When Lolita ruffled her feathers, he jumped again.

"Don't, you're gonna scare her."

"Scare *her*?"

"Be still. I'm serious. If she gets frightened…." Ellie raised her up from her lap. "Be still." Lolita instinctively wrapped her talons around the side of Ellie's hand, then with a shudder, extended her wings and fluttered them up and down. Diablo could barely keep his eyes on the road, between worrying the bird was going to start flying around the inside of the car, to his fascination of her, her wing span, her size, her sheer beauty.

"Wow," was all he could say.

Ellie lowered her slowly, and cradled her in her hands. "It's not far now. Take a right at the next light." By the time Diablo turned into the drive at the nursing home and parked, Lolita was fidgety. She'd even pecked at Ellie several times. Ellie scolded her and smiled. "Is that the thanks I get for saving your life?"

Diablo came around to open her door and stood back. Gripping the side of Ellie's hand, Lolita tested her wings again, fluttering, reaching, cocking her head one way and then the other, hesitating. Then seemingly without effort and with a magnificent wing display, she took flight and disappeared into the night.

Ellie and Diablo hurried inside and rushed down the hall. Grandma Betty looked up when they entered the room and sighed. "Oh good, you're here. I'm so weak, Ellie. I didn't know I'd be this weak." They had removed the IV and at her request, she was wearing her favorite red pantsuit. "How do I look?"

"You look beautiful, Grandma." Ellie kissed her forehead and sat down next to her.

"How's my hair?"

"Perfect," Ellie said, her chin quivering.

"I wish I didn't have to die here."

"I know."

"We had such fun, didn't we?"

"Yes."

"Can I go back outside?" she asked, her chest heaving with each breath. "Do you think they'd let me go outside?"

Ellie's mind raced. "I'll go find out."

A nurse met her coming out of the room, listened to her request, and shook her head. "Not a good idea. We're shorthanded," she said. "Someone would have to go get the key to the back door, move furniture, maneuver the beds...."

"Do you think she could sit up in a wheelchair?" Ellie asked.

Grandma Betty heard. "I can try," she said, barely able to hold her head up.

"There are loungers out there, if we could only get her outside."

"Why don't I just carry her?" Diablo suggested. "Is it all right if I carry her?"

The nurse hesitated, perhaps running through a mental list of rules and regulations, ifs, ands and buts. "Yes."

They moved quickly. "Oh, isn't this grand," Grandma Betty said, as Diablo scooped her up. "I feel like Scarlett O'Hara."

Ellie laughed, gathering up her patchwork-quilt and pillow. "Let's go."

"Wait. I need to say good-bye to April. April, it's time to say good-bye, Okay?"

"Okay," April said. "I'll miss you."

This was it, the sum of their year and a half together as roommates, hardly ever communicating, hardly ever acknowledging one another. They passed by Mary's room, the hypochondriac. "Where you going?" she asked.

"I'm going outside to die," Grandma Betty said.

"Who's that carrying you?"

"This is Diablo. He's very strong. Bye, Mary."

The nurse appeared with the key to the door, extra pillows, and led the way, Ellie at their side.

"Your father just phoned. He said he'd be here within the hour."

Ellie looked at the nurse. Did they have an hour?

Apparently not. The woman shook her head. Down the main corridor, they passed two more residents. Grandma Betty told them both good-bye as well, even though she'd never met the two women. Every aide and nurse they encountered, she bid farewell also.

The nurse unlocked the door and they stepped out into the night. She and Ellie positioned the pillows on the lounger then covered them with the patchwork-quilt. Diablo set Grandma Betty down gently and the nurse and Ellie fussed making her comfortable. "Thank you," she said, all situated. "This is nice. Thank you." The night air was warm, with a soft breeze, not a cloud in the sky. Faces and voices blended in the darkness.

She could hear her favorite aide, "I come to say good-bye, Betty." A kiss on her cheek.

"Me, too," Sophie said.

"Betty, are you in pain?"

"No, Mary, it's not bad at all."

"Mr. Cooper says good-bye. He's sitting by his window."

"Betty, wave. April's waving to you." April stood just inside the door, trembling and with big tears in her eyes. She'd rung the buzzer again and again, and insisted on coming.

Grandma Betty waved to her.

"Are you afraid?"

"No. Not at all."

Ellie tucked the quilt around her grandmother's shoulders. She'd paled and was starting to shiver. "You are so sweet," Grandma Betty said, a flicker of sadness crossing her eyes. Ellie was so precious to her. So very precious. "Diablo."

"Yes," he said, down on one knee at her side.

"You take care of her."

"I will."

"Let her take care of you, too."

"I'll try," he said, his voice cracking.

Grandma Betty nodded, her hand soft in Ellie's, her strength failing. "I'll miss you, Ellie."

"Me, too, Grandma," she said, and apologized for crying. "I'm sorry. "

"It's okay." Grandma Betty brought Ellie's hand to her lips. "It's okay."

Ellie looked at Diablo, her heart breaking, a part of her slipping away...then gazed up into the night, tears trickling down her face. "Which star is ours, Grandma?" she asked.

Grandma Betty scanned the darkness, darkness everywhere. "That one right there." She pointed to it, smiling. "That one right there," she said. Then she closed her eyes and in an instant, she was gone.

"Oh, God." Ellie laid her head in her grandmother's lap and hugged her dearly. As a child she would fall asleep like this - so safe, so warm in her grandmother's lap. "Good-bye, Grandma," she said. "I love you." All around them, in the trees and on the rooftops, was the whisper of wings. "I will always love you."

<h1 style="text-align:center">~ 25 ~</h1>

Ellie packed her grandmother's things. April was asleep, her hearing aids removed.

"Is that it?" Diablo asked.

She nodded. Two bags of clothing. "Take them to the Goodwill," her grandmother had said. She'd take them in the morning. Ellie glanced around the room. The bed had been stripped already. A bare mattress, lying flat. She stopped at the nurses' station, went through the motions. "My dad'll have someone pick up the fridge and chair tomorrow."

He and Jewel had just left. The four of them had waited until the undertaker came and went. Ellie insisted Grandma Betty not be brought back inside. Her dad tipped the driver for being so congenial. "Just a little something," he said, to thank the man.

"If anyone wants what's in there...."

The nurse nodded. "You were good to your grandmother," she said.

Ellie looked at her, bottom lip trembling. "Thank you. She wasn't just my Grandma, she was my friend."

"I know." The nurse wrapped her arms around her and squeezed her tight. "Let me give you some advice," she said, breaking down and crying. "Leave this place behind you and don't look back. You did all you could."

"Thank you." Ellie welcomed the woman's touch, her strength, her shoulder to lean on. And when she and Diablo left, she did just that. She left the place behind.

"Where do you want to go?" Diablo asked. "Your apartment or mine?"

"Neither. The night's too pretty," she said.

Diablo smiled, and leaned over and kissed her. "Well, we have to go somewhere. I have to take care of you, you know."

"Oh, God!" Ellie laughed, wiping her eyes. "Leave it to my Grandma."

Diablo chuckled, the two of them gazing at one another. "How about we go get the Harley?"

"Don't you have to work?"

"No, I called off," he said. The night was theirs. They took to the highway, the streets, Diablo's domain. And in the morning, Ellie slept. And slept and slept and slept. When she finally woke, she found she had changed. Her life would never be the same. She'd lost a part of herself, and yet in some ways, she felt richer, more whole, blessed.

Diablo still recognized her. Abby, too.

"What do you mean? Changed how?"

"I don't know," Ellie said, as she and Abby entered the barn. "I have no more secrets. No fear of being different. We're all different. My happiness isn't out there somewhere; it's in here. It's in me."

Abby smiled. "Does this mean we're not going to the Healing Light Symposium this weekend?"

"No, we'll go." Ellie laughed. "I'll just be going for a different reason."

"Which is?"

"Just for the fun of it. The joy of living."

Damian nickered at the sound of her voice.

* * *

Ellie had to go down to the police station and make a statement. As suspected, from his comments, Victor *had* entered her apartment. His fingerprints were all over the place, and her telephone cord, cut. There were no signs of forcible entry. Ellie had been in the habit of hanging her keys on a hook by Damian's stall when she rode, and usually would ride for an hour or so. Apparently Victor took the opportunity to have a key made. Items of her undergarments were also found hidden in his truck.

Why her? Why single her out? She had no answers for the officer.

"And if not you, do you think he would have stalked someone else?"

Ellie refused to even speculate. She shuddered to think. There were generations of women at the barn, little girls like Julie, mothers, daughters, sisters, wives. They were everywhere. Ellie stood. "Can I go now?"

The Saturday following Grandma Betty's death, Ellie and Diablo took to the highway again. As she'd promised, they went as far as they could go in a day. Lolita followed them, as did most of the flock. Diablo looked up into the sky. They were soaring overhead. It was dusk.

"Do you know them all by name?"

Ellie smiled. "No, just Lolita."

Diablo found comfort in that. After all, a pet crow wasn't so weird. Was it? He counted; there had to be at least forty of them settling in the trees.

Ellie opened Grandma Betty's urn, bright red in color, and stared at the contents for a moment.

Diablo expected sadness. He expected tears. He was pleasantly surprised. Ellie walked to the edge of the riverbank and smiled. She could hear her Grandmother's voice in the wind as she scattered the ashes. "Remember, dear...no regrets." She had none.